RACE AGAINST TIME™

Journey to Atlantis

J. J. Fortune

First published in the U.S.A. in 1985
by Dell Publishing Co. Inc., New York
First published in the U.K. in Armada
in 1986 by Fontana Paperbacks,
8 Grafton Street, London W1X 3LA

Armada is an imprint of Fontana Paperbacks,
part of the Collins Publishing Group

Illustrations by Bill Sienkiewicz
Map by Giorgetta Bell McRee

Made and printed in Great Britain by
William Collins Sons & Co. Ltd, Glasgow

BACKS TO THE WALL

None of them were ready for the voice that called into the cave.

"Come out with your hands up."

Stephen tried to place the voice, but he couldn't, even when it continued. "And bring the sacred double-headed ax with you."

Only when they emerged into the sunlight, with Uncle Richard holding the ax high in one hand, could Stephen identify the man who had rescued them.

The leader of HATE.

With him were at least twenty heavily armed men.

"I'll return one art treasure to you now," said Uncle Richard, swinging the golden ax. "Here, catch!"

Race Against Time

Also available in Armada

1. Revenge in the Silent Tomb
2. Escape from Raven Castle
3. Evil in Paradise
4. Search for Mad Jack's Crown
5. Duel for the Samurai Sword
6. Pursuit of the Deadly Diamonds
7. The Secret of the Third Watch
8. Trapped in the U.S.S.R.

Watch out for DANGER: DUE NORTH on sale now!

Special thanks to
Olga Litowinsky, George Nicholson, Bruce Hall,
Betsy Gould, Beverly Horowitz and Helene Steinhauer
from J.J. Fortune and Others.

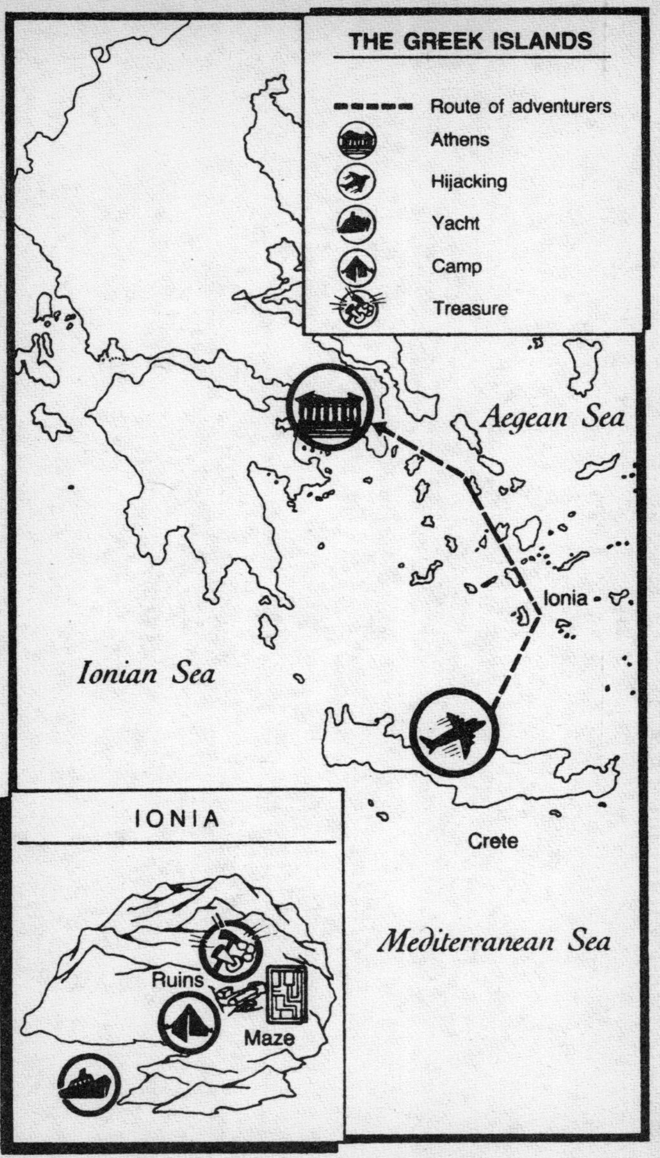
THE GREEK ISLANDS
Route of adventurers
Athens
Hijacking
Yacht
Camp
Treasure
Aegean Sea
Ionia
Ionian Sea
Crete
Mediterranean Sea
IONIA
Ruins
Maze

CONTENTS

1

FIRST-CLASS TERROR

MONDAY: 9:00 A.M.
Somewhere Over the Mediterranean

"Just an hour and a half before we land in Athens," Stephen Lane said to Uncle Richard after a quick glance at his Kronom watch.

"Not a bad flight at all," said Uncle Richard. He stretched in his roomy airline seat, unkinking the muscles in his long, lean, athletic body. "Flying first class is worth it for the comfort—though you needn't mention our first-class tickets to your dad. He might consider it a wasteful extravagance. Part of his being a good investment banker, I suppose."

Uncle Richard glanced across the aisle, as he had a number of times during the flight.

"Now, there's someone who really knows how to take advantage of going first class," he said.

Sitting across the aisle was a young woman with long blond hair. Her bright red mouth was pursed in delicious anticipation as a flight attendant popped the cork of a champagne bottle while another flight attendant set down a plate of gleaming gray caviar.

She took a delicate first sip of the foaming liquid, then put on a pair of oversized glasses to read the label on the bottle. Stephen saw an amazing transformation. It reminded him of old movies he had seen, but in reverse. When this woman put on glasses she turned from a foolishly pretty twenty-one-year-old to a striking, keenly intelligent woman of perhaps twenty-eight.

Uncle Richard saw what Stephen did. He leaned toward her to start a conversation, when a loud, harsh voice booming over the plane's public address system froze him and everyone else in the first-class section.

First the voice spoke in Greek, then in heavily accented English.

"Attention. Attention all passengers. Please pay attention and follow all directions for your own safety."

"Oh, dear," said the woman across the aisle to Uncle Richard. "I'm sure they're going to announce rough weather. There goes my champagne, unless I want to gulp it. And it's an absolute sin to gulp really good champagne."

But the voice on the loudspeaker was announcing something far rougher than a storm.

"This is to inform you that this airliner and everyone aboard is now under the command of the Hellenic Alliance to Terminate Exploitation, otherwise known as HATE. We are well-armed and not afraid to do anything that will further our just and noble cause. The pilot and co-pilot are under our guns. All flight personnel are bound and gagged. And in a moment members of our group will come among you requesting contributions to our treasury—generous contributions, please. Do not resist, or you will suffer the penalty. In a short time we will inform you of the plane's new destination. Long live our great nation and its glorious heritage!"

The voice went silent in a screech of static. Then the cockpit door opened and three skyjackers emerged. Two were small and dark and carried revolvers. The third was a tall man with a pale face and bright red hair. He carried a long, wicked-looking knife.

"Let me introduce myself," the red-haired man said. "I go by the name of Zeus, the chief of the ancient gods who were worshipped when our land was truly great. Soon those gods will be worshipped again, when Greece is great once more."

The skyjackers had no trouble collecting "contributions." Passengers were holding out handfuls of currency before they were asked. Some were offering credit cards. The threat on the skyjackers' faces was even more chilling than the deadly weapons in their hands.

When they reached Stephen and Uncle Richard, Stephen went rigid with dread at the gleam of the insane rage in Zeus's eyes.

Then he saw that the tall man with the knife wasn't looking at him or Uncle Richard.

Zeus was looking down at the young blond woman, who was looking up at him, her blue eyes huge with fear behind her glasses.

"Your name?" the tall man asked.

"Diana Briggs," she said. Her knuckles went white as they tightened around the stem of her champagne glass.

"Good," said Zeus. "I'm glad you didn't try to lie about it. Not that it would have done you any good. We were overjoyed when we found your name on the passenger list. We were planning to seize the plane anyway, but having you aboard is a wonderful bonus."

"Me?" said Diana. "Why me? I've done nothing."

"You'll find out your crime when I inflict the punishment," said the man. "But first we'll celebrate our triumph." He lifted the champagne bottle to his lips and took a long swig. Then, wiping his lips on the back of his knife hand, he passed the bottle to his companions. It took the three skyjackers just two turns apiece to finish the bottle.

"And now for serious business," said Zeus, his eyes gleaming even more brightly now.

With a sudden brutal gesture he grabbed Diana's

hair with one hand, jerking her head back so that her white throat was exposed.

The knife in the man's other hand was poised to do its terrifying work.

"You can't—" said Uncle Richard, starting to rise from his seat, only to be stopped by a revolver pointed straight at his forehead.

"You'll soon see just what we can do," said Zeus. "First to Miss Briggs here. And then to any other passengers who might think of resisting."

Uncle Richard could only sit gripping the arms of his seat in helpless anger as Zeus prepared to use his knife on Diana Briggs.

Between clenched teeth Uncle Richard muttered, "It's a nightmare. . . ."

2

A DREAM OF A TRIP

THURSDAY: 8:00 P.M.
New York City

Danger was the furthest thing from anyone's mind the night that Uncle Richard first announced he had been invited to Greece.

It was eight P.M. on a Thursday, three days before the flight to Athens. The Lanes and Uncle Richard had just sat down to dinner, which was usually served that late in the Lanes' Upper East Side Manhattan home. It gave Mr. Lane a chance to get a few extra hours work done in his office far downtown in the Wall Street financial district. And it let Mrs. Lane finish up a full day at her mid-Manhattan health-food store, Oh, Nuts! and still have time to indulge in her second favorite activity, creative cooking.

Tonight as a special treat Mrs. Lane had concocted a dish that she called "nouvelle Japanese." It was made up of a number of vegetables that Stephen had no hope of identifying as he shoveled them into his mouth along with heaps of brown rice. He was using chopsticks, as did everyone at the table but his father.

Mr. Lane was inspecting the pale yellow vegetable on his fork.

"Actually," he said, "I'm not terribly hungry tonight. Had a big business lunch."

"Oh, just come right out and say you don't like it, James," said Mrs. Lane.

"Not at all, dear," said Mr. Lane. "In fact, I find it quite delicious. But I do have to cut down on my meals. I'm starting to put on a few extra pounds, and the tennis season is coming up. I don't want to disgrace myself in my Sunday doubles game."

"How do you like it, Richard?" Mrs. Lane asked her brother.

"Superb. You're not only beautiful, bright, and efficient—you're also a great cook," said Uncle Richard with a grin.

"You should save that line of flattery for the woman you plan to marry—if you ever succeed in finding her," said Mrs. Lane. "And what about you, Stephen?"

"I figure I should start shaving first," said Stephen, grinning too.

"I mean the *food*," said his mother.

"Great," Stephen said between mouthfuls. "I'm starving. Rough afternoon on the ball field. We had to go twelve innings to win."

"Try not to wolf down your food," his mother told him. "You should try to pay attention to the various ethnic cuisines I prepare. A country's food has a great deal to tell you about the flavor of its life and culture. It's one of the best ways to learn about foreign lands, short of going to them, of course."

"What about Greece?" said Uncle Richard out of the blue.

Mrs. Lane looked at him, a bit startled.

"Well, they do have very nourishing salads, and yogurt and honey," she said. "I must say, though, I find their use of olive oil a little too—"

"I don't mean that," said Uncle Richard. "I mean, how would you like it if Stephen and I went there next week?"

Stephen looked up from his food. This was the first he had heard about Uncle Richard's plan. And why was Uncle Richard actually telling his parents about it?

"This is an exceptional opportunity," Uncle Richard went on. "I just received a letter from an old friend, Constantine Andropolis, inviting me to visit a new villa he's moved into outside Athens. I once helped him out of a little difficulty a few years ago, and Greeks tend to be passionate about repaying debts as well as being famous for their hospitality.

I'm positive that he'd welcome having Stephen come with me."

"I must say, this is rather sudden," said Mr. Lane. "Such a long trip on such short notice. And during the school year as well."

"Not a long trip at all, just nine hours by jet," said Uncle Richard. "And think of the educational value. Stephen can visit the Acropolis and the great national Archaeological Museum. Then it's not too far from Athens to Delphi, where the famous oracle was, and to Mount Olympus. That's not to mention modern Greece and all that Stephen can learn about it. As a bonus, my friend Constantine is an expert on Greek antiquities *and* current Greek affairs, and loves to share his knowledge about both."

Stephen still had no idea what was behind Uncle Richard's scheme. He said, "Right now we're studying ancient civilizations in my history class. I'd bet anything that my teacher would give me extra credit for a trip to Greece, just as long as I wrote a report on what I see and learn there. I mean, last year, when we were studying American history, Jimmy Squires got credit for a report he did on his trip to see the exhibits at Disneyland. And I wouldn't be seeing imitations of the past; I'd be seeing the real thing. It would probably even raise my grade."

"Besides, we can go at bargain off-season rates," said Uncle Richard to Mr. Lane. "It's really an excellent investment in Stephen's future."

''Well, looking at it that way . . .'' said Mr. Lane, weakening.

''I'm not sure Stephen is old enough to go to such a foreign place,'' said Mrs. Lane. ''There would be so much that is so strange to him; all kinds of accidents could happen.''

''But I'll be with him all the time,'' said Uncle Richard. ''And you have to admit, Marion, that in all the other times you've left me in charge of Stephen, absolutely nothing dangerous has happened to him. In fact, I'm afraid Stephen has been a bit bored by my refusal to let him do anything at all risky. But you know me, safety always comes first.''

''Please let me go,'' said Stephen to his parents. ''I promise to write a super report. And I won't bug Uncle Richard to do anything he doesn't want us to do.''

''What about homework from this week?'' asked Mr. Lane.

''We wouldn't be leaving until Sunday night,'' said Uncle Richard. ''Stephen can get it all done before we go.''

''*Please,*'' said Stephen.

''I must admit, fares are a real bargain this time of year,'' said Mr. Lane. ''Costwise, the project does make sense.''

''And it would be an enriching experience,'' said Mrs. Lane.

''Then the answer is yes?'' said Uncle Richard.

''If he does all his homework, including any extra his teachers may assign, before he leaves,'' said Mr. Lane. ''And if he promises to turn in a really solid report.''

''And if he takes his vitamins regularly, and you, Richard, give your word that he will get enough sleep and stay out of the noontime sun and won't try to do too much too fast,'' said Mrs. Lane. ''Then I suppose we'd have to agree.''

''I can promise you,'' said Uncle Richard, ''that Stephen will be as safe from harm as he's always been with me.''

''Well, we can't ask for more than that,'' said Mrs. Lane.

''Just as long as you don't let Stephen lead you astray, Richard,'' said Mr. Lane, chuckling at his own little joke, and pleased to see that both Stephen and Uncle Richard seemed to appreciate the humor as well.

After dinner Stephen went up to the top floor apartment that Uncle Richard occupied in the Lanes' brownstone. It was decorated with souvenirs from Uncle Richard's travels as an engineer—Japanese screens, Russian samovars, fine French porcelain, African witch doctor masks, and more. Only Stephen and Uncle Richard knew about the array of weapons concealed in the room, just as only they knew about the collection of souvenirs that Stephen had hidden in his room, mementos of past dangers that he and Uncle Richard had shared and survived.

Ever since Uncle Richard had come to live at the Lanes' home, after retiring with a tidy fortune at the age of thirty-three, Stephen had been secretly going with him on adventures all around the world. Stephen and Uncle Richard had agreed there was no reason to cause Stephen's parents unnecessary alarm by mentioning their trips. Besides, it would have ended the uncle and nephew's fun together.

"I was wondering how long it would be before I had to take my Kronom out of hiding," Stephen said to Uncle Richard.

He picked up his Kronom K-D2 wristwatch. It was a marvel of electronic technology that had countless uses, from serving as a computer to acting as a weapon. Stephen and Uncle Richard each had one, and these watches had saved them from disaster many times.

"What's waiting for us in Athens?" Stephen asked. "Blackmail? Theft? Espionage? Counterfeiting? Murder?"

"Nothing," said Uncle Richard.

"*Nothing?*" said Stephen.

"Absolutely nothing—except what I told your parents," said Uncle Richard. "My old friend Constantine invited me to visit his new villa and he'll be happy to have you come too. It's been too long since I took a nice relaxed trip, and it's about time I did something about furthering your education instead of leading you into tight spots.''

''Then I won't have to take my Kronom along,'' Stephen said. He did not know whether to feel relieved or disappointed. Going on an adventure with Uncle Richard was always exciting but often too scary for comfort, like going on a roller coaster with no guarantee that the car wouldn't go flying off the tracks.

''Of course you should take it along,'' said Uncle Richard. ''You can use it for measuring the heights of ancient columns. Or for finding the proportions of statues. Or for carbon-dating artifacts. Or for translating inscriptions. But this time the one thing you won't have to use it for is to save your life. I can feel it in my bones—this trip is going to go smooth as a dream.''

3

ROUGH LANDING

MONDAY: 9:32 A.M.
Crete

Now, eight hours after takeoff from Kennedy Airport in New York, the dream trip had turned into a nightmare.

Zeus stood with one hand pulling back Diana Briggs's head by her long blond hair, and the other hand threatening her with a razor-edged knife.

All Diana could do was gasp out, "But what do you have against me?"

"You are an archaeologist, are you not, Miss Briggs?" Zeus said.

"Why, yes," said Diana. "But how did you know? And what does that have to do with this?"

"Our organization has many members who know a

great deal about your profession,'' Zeus said. ''Your name was recognized immediately, since I myself have read several articles you have written for professional journals.''

''I suppose I should feel flattered,'' said Diana. ''But somehow I don't exactly think you're a fan of mine.''

Then she gave a cry of pain as the skyjacker gave a short, sharp tug at her hair.

''This is nothing to what you can expect,'' the skyjacker said. ''You're a gift sent to us by the ancient Greek gods. We've seized this plane to protest the looting of the treasures of the Greek past by foreign archaeologists. Many years ago you archaeologists shipped our best statues and other works of art back to your own countries for your own museums and millionaire collectors. Today, though officially such acts are forbidden, we know that the same kind of thievery still goes on, and our government does not allot sufficient men or money to stop it.''

''I have nothing to do with that,'' said Diana.

''That doesn't matter,'' said Zeus. ''You're just a symbol, and what we'll do to you will be a symbolic act.''

''And what will that be?'' said Diana, unable to keep the terror out of her voice.

''I'm about to do to you what patriots did to women who collaborated with the enemy during World War Two,'' Zeus said. ''I will hack your hair off so that all that remains is a stubble to signify your shame.''

''And after I just spent fifty dollars for a super-stylish cut,'' said Diana, and gasped again at another tug of her hair.

''I will now begin,'' said Zeus, and laid the edge of his knife alongside the hair he was grasping.

''Wait a minute!'' Uncle Richard said sharply. Zeus turned his head to look angrily at him.

''This is your last warning, Mr. American Nice Guy,'' Zeus said. ''Stay out of this business that does not concern you or what will happen to you will be no symbolic act. It will be for real.''

''You've got me wrong,'' said Uncle Richard. ''I want to help you. You see, I sympathize with your cause. You guys have really something to be angry about. But you're going about it all wrong.''

''What do you mean?'' Zeus said. ''And who are you anyway.''

''Dick Duffy is my name, and P.R.'s my game,'' said Uncle Richard in a hearty tone as different from his normal crisp, cool voice as night from day.

''P.R.?'' said Zeus. ''What does this word mean?''

''Public relations,'' said Uncle Richard. ''The science of getting your point of view across to the public. And let me tell you, as one of the top men in the field, I can say that you fellows need my advice.''

''About what?'' Zeus asked. ''It seems to me we've done very well without your guidance.''

"Up to now," said Uncle Richard. "But stealing a plane and cutting off a woman's hair is one thing—and making it count is another. You have to communicate with the public or your symbolic act will be like tossing a pebble into the sea and watching it disappear. You have to make a big splash."

"A big splash?" Zeus said, doubt entering his voice for the first time.

"Media exposure," said Uncle Richard. "TV cameras, radio interviews, the works. You have to wait to cut off her hair until the plane lands. Then you wait until they can set up the cameras and get the reporters on the scene."

"I hate to admit it, but you may be right," said Zeus, and he loosened his hold on Diana's hair.

Her shoulders sagged with relief until he held the knife blade in front of her face and said, "You can enjoy your expensive haircut for a little while longer, before we give you a free one when we land."

"Incidentally, when will that be?" asked Uncle Richard.

"In two hours, on the island of Crete, near its capital, Iraklion," Zeus said. "You see, even without your advice we know how to gain publicity. Crete was the home of one of the oldest civilizations in the world, the ancient Minoan empire, long before it became part of Greece. We will land there to make our statement about protecting the glorious legacy of the past. Then we will fly on to a country that has promised us sanctuary."

"Hey, you guys are right on the ball," said Uncle Richard. "If you're ever in the Big Apple and want a job, look me up. My profession can always use fresh blood."

"Just make sure you do not try anything foolish," said Zeus, "or yours will be the blood *we* want."

Those menacing words were still echoing in Stephen's memory two hours later when the plane landed on the dusty runway of the Iraklion airport.

Stephen looked out the plane window. He saw ambulances, TV camera trucks, police, army troops, and gaping onlookers.

"As you can see, we've already radioed our demands and instructions to the authorities," said Zeus. "In a short time, as you Americans like to say, we'll be able to get our show on the road."

At that moment a skyjacker carrying a submachine gun emerged from the cockpit and whispered something into Zeus's ear. Zeus grimaced with disgust.

"It seems there'll be a delay," he said. "The TV people inform us by radio that it'll take them several hours to arrange the live TV satellite hook-up we've demanded."

The passengers within earshot groaned, and from economy class came the sound of a screaming baby.

"Perhaps you could untie a couple of the attendants and have them pass out refreshments," suggested Uncle Richard. "You know, keep all the good folks aboard happy."

"I wouldn't mind another bottle of champagne right now," said Diana. "It might dull the pain of what's to come."

"I prefer to keep them tied up," the skyjacker said. "And I don't want to waste any of the water or provisions aboard. We can't be sure how long they'll have to last."

"But you can just order the authorities to bring fresh food and drink to the plane," said Uncle Richard. "They have to do anything you ask."

"Quite right," said Zeus, clearly relishing the idea. He told his confederate, "Go to the radio and command provisions be brought. But warn them not to try any funny business—if they do not want a blood bath."

A half hour later the provisions still had not come.

The red-haired skyjacker barked another command. "Tell them to bring the provisions quickly, or after ten minutes we will begin shooting the passengers one by one."

Stephen looked at his Kronom as the numbers on it changed. One minute. Two minutes. Three minutes. Four minutes. Five minutes. Six minutes. Seven minutes. Eight minutes.

A provision truck began to roll toward the airplane.

"It's about time," Zeus said as the first of the four workmen in badly worn and stained blue jumpsuits began to laboriously haul containers off the truck and stack them beside the plane.

"No, no, you must bring them aboard. Don't expect us to do your work for you."

A gangway was wheeled to the plane door, and the workmen started carrying containers aboard, grunting and straining under their loads.

The first three passed through the first-class section on their way to the economy class. Zeus stopped the fourth with the palm of his hand against the short, barrel-shaped man's chest.

"You've gone far enough," Zeus said. "We'll take what you have here, and it had better be good."

"Yes, sir. Of course, sir," said the workman, stooping to put his container down. "Just take a look at this, sir. I am sure, sir, that it will please you."

Zeus and his two companions bent over to get a good view. Suddenly the workman stood up, a can in his hand spraying blinding liquid in the skyjackers' faces.

At the same time Uncle Richard leaped up from his seat, grabbed a revolver from one of the blinded men's hands, and raced to the cockpit door. He flung it open and shouted to the other skyjackers within, "Drop your guns. It's all over."

And it was. The workmen in economy class had done their work just as efficiently.

"Thanks for your help, Richard," the barrel-shaped man in first class said after the skyjackers, their vision still blurred, had been led away. "As soon as I saw your name on the passenger list, I knew I could count on you."

"And as soon as I saw your face coming through the door, I knew our troubles were over," said Uncle Richard, clasping the man's hand.

Then Uncle Richard turned to Stephen and said, "Let me introduce an old friend of mine. You've already heard his name, and I told you what a help he'd be when we arrived. Steve, meet Constantine Andropolis."

4

A RISKY PROPOSITION

MONDAY: 2:11 P.M.
Crete

"See that fountain with the stone lions?" asked Constantine Andropolis.

It was three hours after the hijacking, and Stephen and Uncle Richard were sitting with Constantine at an outdoor café in Iraklion.

"It looks really old," said Stephen, looking across the square to the time-weathered fountain that Constantine had pointed out.

"Over five hundred years old, built by the Venetians when Crete was part of their empire," said Constantine. "On Crete, that is almost new. Over a thousand years before the Venetians, the Greeks and then the Romans ruled the island. And over a thousand years before *them,* Crete was the center of the great Minoan civilization that flourished here and on some of the islands to the north. Perhaps you will visit the ruins of the great Minoan palace of Knossos, just a few miles from Iraklion, and one of the wonders of the ages.''

''I told you that Constantine was an expert on antiquities,'' said Uncle Richard, taking a sip of the thick black coffee that he and Constantine were drinking.

''A Greek has to be interested in the past; it is always around him,'' said Constantine. ''Even when I drink this coffee I remember it was brought here by the Turks when they took the island from the Venetians. Perhaps you would like a taste?''

''Thanks, but I'll stick to my Coca-Cola,'' said Stephen.

''Of course, young people, especially Americans, prefer to live in the present,'' said Constantine, smiling. ''I, too, whether I like it or not, must live most of my time in the present—as you saw today. It is an inescapable part of my job.''

''What is your job anyway?'' asked Stephen.

''Didn't Richard tell you?''

Uncle Richard cleared his throat uncomfortably and took a sip of the ice water that was served with the coffee.

''I didn't think it was, er, necessary,'' he said. ''You did write that you would be on vacation, and I didn't think your job would come up. I guess I should tell you now, Steve, that Constantine is head of the anti-art-smuggling division of the International Police Organization—Interpol."

"My vacation was over almost before it began," said Constantine. "I was rushed to Crete to try to talk the skyjackers out of their plan. But when they asked for provisions to be brought to them, the opportunity for direct action was too good to be missed. Especially when I found out you were aboard, Richard. I still remember the time you saved my life from those Egyptian tomb thieves."

"You more than evened the score today," said Uncle Richard. "In fact, now I owe you a favor."

Hearing those words, Constantine stopped smiling. His face and voice were all business.

"I was hoping you'd say that, Richard. There is a favor you can do for me. A very big favor. But, unfortunately, a very dangerous one."

Stephen recognized the gleam that appeared in Uncle Richard's eyes. It reminded him of the gleam that had been sparked when Uncle Richard spotted Diana Briggs on the plane. It was much more intense though. At times Uncle Richard might be able to resist a pretty woman, but never the promise of an adventure spiced with risk.

"What's up?" Uncle Richard asked.

"Perhaps nothing," said Constantine. "But I must be sure. Too much is at stake."

"How much?" asked Uncle Richard.

"A treasure. A treasure beyond our wildest dreams. A treasure that would make men commit any crime to get at—including murder."

"Tell me more," said Uncle Richard, leaning forward.

"You know, of course, the legend of Atlantis," said Constantine, "the fabulously rich and civilized continent that was swallowed by the sea. You doubtless also know that we now think that Atlantis actually existed."

"Right," said Uncle Richard, "except it wasn't a continent but an island. The island of Santorini, less than fifty miles from Crete." He turned to Stephen to give him a full explanation.

"Thirty-five hundred years ago, over half of Santorini was destroyed by one of the greatest volcanic explosions in recorded history. That explosion darkened the skies of the world. It set off a rain of ashes and a giant tidal wave that destroyed Minoan civilization not only on Santorini but on Crete and other islands as well, if you can imagine such a cataclysm."

"I can imagine it," said Stephen. "I remember that tidal wave we saw in Hawaii and what it could do."

Stephen was talking about the tidal wave that had capped their adventure in *Evil in Paradise*. When

Constantine looked interested, Stephen got ready to tell him the story.

But Uncle Richard wasn't interested in looking backward, not with a fresh challenge ahead.

Eagerly he asked Constantine, "And now somebody has solved the mystery of the lost treasure of Atlantis?"

"What lost treasure?" asked Stephen.

"On Santorini archaeologists have unearthed splendid buildings and beautiful wall paintings and superb pottery, but not a trace of precious metals or jewels," Uncle Richard explained.

"We think that the population was warned by earth tremors of the approaching catastrophe, and fled the island with all their valuables. But where they went has remained a mystery until now." He turned to Constantine. "Who's found it?"

"Professor Sophocles Democrites, the most famous archaeologist in Greece," said Constantine. "For the past two years he has been commanding an excavation on an uninhabited island called Ionia. He has refused to let anyone know what he is looking for, since he despises vulgar publicity. Because of his immense prestige the authorities agreed to his demand that they keep their distance.

"I, however, took the precaution of hiring an informant among his workmen. Two days ago the man radioed me that the first traces of treasure had been found. Then the radio went dead. I don't have to tell you what I fear, or that I need someone to find out what happened and take the right steps."

"You've just found him," said Uncle Richard.

"The only problem is, we need a reason for you to be on the island," said Constantine. "The professor won't let any outsiders get near the place."

Uncle Richard's face darkened with thought as he looked into the dregs of his coffee. Then he brightened.

"I've got a plan!" he announced.

Stephen leaned forward. Even though Uncle Richard's plans didn't always exactly work, they were always interesting.

"I could pretend to be an archaeologist," Uncle Richard said. "If the professor is a true scientist, he won't want to keep secrets from other members of the scientific community."

"Good plan," approved Constantine. "By a stroke of luck the professor is here on Crete now and is due to sail to his island of mystery tomorrow. I can introduce you to him and vouch for your credentials this very night. There's a good chance he'll say yes when you ask if he'll take you with him."

"Of course, that leaves Steve to be accounted for," said Uncle Richard. "Perhaps, Constantine, you could take him to Athens and show him the sights while I do the job. It shouldn't take long."

"Uncle Richard," Stephen protested. "*You're* supposed to take care of me. Besides, who would take

care of *you* if you get in a jam? Remember how I've helped you before."

"But what about that school report you're supposed to write?" said Uncle Richard.

"Come *on*, Uncle Richard," said Stephen. "I *know* you'll be able to come up with a plan to solve a little problem like that."

"It might not be a bad idea to have you along," said Uncle Richard as Stephen was sure he would. "The professor wouldn't object to having a youngster fascinated with archaeology along. And it would help dispel any suspicion about me. Who would think that a man on a dangerous mission would take his nephew along?"

Uncle Richard paused, then added hastily, "Not that I think there's going to be much danger, you understand. I think you've exaggerated that part, Constantine. Personally, I don't see any serious trouble ahead."

At that moment Constantine shouted, "Quick! Dive under the table!"

5

A HOT TIME IN THE OLD TOWN

MONDAY: 3:00 P.M.
Crete

Uncle Richard, Stephen, and Constantine met under the café table as a deafening explosion shattered the air. A bomb had gone off.

A split second later Constantine was out from under the table with his revolver drawn and firing at a speeding car that was just turning out of the square.

"I think I hit a tire," said Constantine, running toward the sound of a crash. Uncle Richard and Stephen followed on his heels.

When they turned the corner they saw the car smashed against the side of a building.

Three men were running at full speed away from the wreck.

"After them!" shouted Constantine.

They tore after the fleeing men down a long street lined with tourist shops and travel agencies.

"We've got them now," said Constantine as they emerged onto the harbor front and saw the men running onto a narrow causeway that led to a huge stone fort.

A group of tourists froze with surprise as the men went past them through the fort entrance and Constantine, Uncle Richard, and Stephen followed a few seconds later.

"Which way did they go?" said Uncle Richard, peering around him in the vast, dimly lit interior lined with weapons of the past—swords and spears, blunderbusses, and cannon.

Suddenly there was the sound of a modern weapon—a revolver, echoing loudly.

Constantine turned, his gun pointed up the narrow stone stairway from which the shot had come. A voice behind him said, "Drop your pistol and raise your hands, all three of you."

A man with a drawn gun emerged from the dark corner where he had been hiding.

"You captured our leader," he said. "And now you will pay the penalty."

"You're part of HATE?" said Uncle Richard.

"You're very smart," said the terrorist, "for someone so stupid. We've led you into this trap. And now we will close its jaws on you." He gave a loud whistle.

Another terrorist emerged from the shadows on the other side of the room while the third came down the stone stairway.

The first terrorist stooped and picked up Constantine's revolver.

"Thank you very much for this contribution to our arsenal," the man said. "Let me assure you, it will be used for a good cause. The elimination of enemies like you."

He put his own pistol into his pocket and pointed Constantine's at him.

"You can say good-bye to life," said the terrorist. "We sentence you and your allies here to death as traitors to the cause of the restoration of ancient Greek glory."

"I insist that you shoot me first," Uncle Richard said. "I'm the worst of the lot. I'm the one who really put your leader behind bars."

"If you insist, then I will be only too happy to—" the terrorist began.

He stopped in mid-sentence as Uncle Richard rushed him.

He frantically squeezed the trigger of his gun.

Nothing happened.

And before the terrorist could get out his own pistol, Uncle Richard's fist was crashing against his jaw.

Almost in the same motion Uncle Richard reached into the man's pocket for his pistol.

The other two terrorists didn't wait for him to get it. They started running for the stairway.

Grabbing a spear, Stephen thrust it between one man's legs as he raced past him.

The effect was more spectacular than Stephen had dared hope.

His hands waving wildly, the man went flying through the air. His head collided with the rough stone wall, and he fell in an unconscious heap.

"Only one more to go!" said Uncle Richard, leading the way up the stone steps. Stephen followed close behind, with Constantine a close third.

They climbed out to the roof of the fort, blinking in the dazzling afternoon sunlight.

"Uncle Richard, look out!" Stephen shouted.

The third terrorist emerged from behind a large pyramid of cannonballs. He hurled himself at Uncle Richard.

Uncle Richard wheeled around to face him. Sidestepping, he grabbed the man's hand and flipped him into the air and over the rampart of the fort.

Constantine and Stephen joined Uncle Richard at the rampart to look down at the crumpled figure of the man on the rocks below. Luckily for him, he wasn't killed, just knocked cold. The police could come and cart him away.

6

MR. MONEY AND HIS MEN

TUESDAY: 6:20 A.M.
Crete

The sun was just clearing the horizon as Stephen and Uncle Richard walked along the waterfront toward the yacht that would take them to the island of Ionia.

"As I was saying to Constantine before we were so rudely interrupted," said Uncle Richard, "I really don't expect any troub—"

Then he shouted, "Look out!"

He grabbed Stephen's arm and yanked him aside violently. A large crate came crashing down from a towering loading crane.

A man in workman's blue coveralls leaped from the controls of the crane and raced away.

Uncle Richard took a step in pursuit, then stopped himself.

"There's no time to chase him," he said. "The yacht is due to sail with the tide in a few minutes, and we don't want to miss it—as somebody clearly wants us to do."

"What were you saying about no trouble ahead?" said Stephen.

"Move it!" said Uncle Richard, quickening his pace toward where the long white yacht was moored.

A familiar figure was standing and waving at them at the yacht railing. It was Diana Briggs.

"More trouble," said Uncle Richard.

"I see we're traveling together again," Diana said after they joined her on deck. "Let's hope this trip is more peaceful than our last one. But you should have told me you were an archaeologist, Richard. It gives us so much in common."

"Things were too hectic on the plane for me to talk shop," said Uncle Richard, and changed the subject. "So you work for the professor?"

"Indeed I do," said Diana. "In fact, if it weren't for me, we wouldn't be going on this trip at all. It was I who introduced the professor to Mr. Money."

"Mr. Money?" said Uncle Richard.

"That's my name for him because he's financing the project," said Diana. "The professor ran out of money last year, and neither the Greek government nor his university had any aid to give him. Then I remembered this man I had met in New York. His real name is Midas—and it fits. He's one of the most successful art dealers in the world, and filthy rich. He also has a passion for the past, and when I asked him to back the professor, all he asked for in return was the privilege of being on hand when the professor made his great discovery."

"Then they're about to find the treasure?" asked Uncle Richard.

His voice was too eager. Diana gave him a questioning look before she replied. "Perhaps. We can't be sure, of course. You must know that quite well, as an archaeologist."

"Of course," said Uncle Richard quickly, and was spared further embarrassment when a crewman on the pier cast off the line that moored the ship.

The yacht's powerful engine throbbed. The crewman jumped aboard, and the yacht headed out toward the open sea, past the huge Venetian fort that once had guarded the harbor from Turkish pirates and yesterday had been the scene of Uncle Richard and Stephen's fight for their lives.

Above, the sky had turned the most intense blue Stephen had ever seen. Below, the sea was an even deeper blue. On the rippling water sunlight exploded like a million flashbulbs as far as the eye could see. Close to the ship's prow a school of dolphins broke the surface, their leaping bodies flashing silver.

"This is the part of a voyage I like best," said Uncle Richard. "The very beginning, when everything ahead is part of the great unknown."

"Why, Mr. Duffy," said Diana, "I do believe you're a romantic."

"Indeed, sir, you are a man after my own heart," said a booming voice behind them. Its accent was not quite British and not quite American. Stephen couldn't decide whether it belonged to the drawing rooms of London or to the streets of the Bronx. "I, too, am a romantic—a romantic to the core. But let me introduce myself. Midas is my name."

When Stephen turned and got his first sight of Midas, he fought to keep his mouth from dropping open in surprise.

There, standing before him in a tentlike white suit, was an immensely fat, bald man—a dead ringer for the actor Sydney Greenstreet in the old movie, *The Maltese Falcon*. Stephen had rented that classic film for his video recorder at home and had watched it three nights in a row when he was supposed to be doing his homework.

Behind Midas were two other men whom Stephen would have much rather met on the screen than in real life.

"Allow me to introduce my associates," said Midas. "First, this is Mr. Apollo, an Athenian businessman who very generously offered to help support the professor's noble work."

"I am happy to help recover the glorious heritage of my beloved nation," said Mr. Apollo in the voice of someone reciting a memorized speech in a language he did not understand. Mr. Apollo was a small, pale man who despite the heat of the day wore a navy blue pinstriped suit with boxlike shoulders. Even so, he looked as cold as ice.

Midas had no such advantage. He pulled out a handkerchief and mopped his dripping forehead before he introduced his other companion.

"This is Mr. Stavros, who heads our labor force."

"Yeah, head of labor force," Mr. Stavros echoed. It was clear he was a man who preferred action to words. His muscles bulged, straining the fabric of his blue and white striped T-shirt and white denim jeans.

"Glad to meet you all," said Uncle Richard. "I'm Richard Duffy, and this is my nephew, Steve. I hope you don't mind having us along."

"Sir, we are delighted to have you," said Midas. "Anything the professor wants is fine with us. We are interested only in furthering his great work."

"By the way, where is the professor?" asked Uncle Richard.

"Resting," said Midas. "He's not as young as he once was, and he'll need all his energy when we reach the island and begin the final phase of this momentous task."

"Then you're near success," said Uncle Richard.

"Perhaps you shouldn't . . ." Diana began to caution Midas.

"Nonsense, my dear," said Midas. "Our two

friends are clearly to be trusted. Besides, there is no way for them to communicate with the outside world."

"Right. We're all in the same boat," said Stephen, and told himself that Uncle Richard and he had to be careful to keep out of sight the powerful radio transmitter that Constantine had given them to call for help if they needed it.

"All in the same boat—how delightfully amusing," said Midas, his vast bulk quivering in a belly laugh. "How I like a lad with a sharp sense of humor! I'm sure we'll get on together famously."

"Maybe I'll follow the professor's example and take a nap," said Uncle Richard. "I want to be wide awake when the action starts."

"Splendid idea, sir," said Midas. "The bunks in your cabin are already made up."

"It's right next to mine," said Diana. "I'll show you the way. I'm turning in myself. I need my beauty sleep."

Diana led Uncle Richard and Stephen belowdecks and down a passageway to their cabin door. Before Uncle Richard opened it, he turned to her and said, "Nice bunch of fellows you're traveling with."

"Mr. Money and his men?" said Diana. "Oh, they might have a few rough spots, but all in all they're perfectly all right." Then she hesitated, and added, "At least I always thought so up until now."

"You have your doubts?" asked Uncle Richard, looking her in the eye.

"Look, I'll level with you if you level with me," said Diana. "You're not really an archaeologist, are you?"

"How did you guess?" said Uncle Richard.

"I'm not as easy to fool as the professor," said Diana. "He might be an expert on the ancient world, but he doesn't know much about the modern one. He's too trusting. Besides, I saw how friendly you were with the man who saved us from the skyjackers, and I know perfectly well who Constantine Andropolis is. You're investigating this project, right?"

"And we need all the help we can get," said Uncle Richard. "After seeing those characters on deck I have a feeling we'll really need it. You can be a big help to us and the professor, Diana, if you tell us what you know."

"I have no proof, but I do have suspicions," said Diana. "Mr. Money and his men have been acting less like generous benefactors as we get closer to the treasure and more like ravenous vultures."

She put her hand on Uncle Richard's arm. "Maybe together we'll be able to stop them. I know we'll make a good team."

"I have the very same feeling," said Uncle Richard, continuing to gaze into her eyes.

"Time for a little shut-eye," said Stephen loudly as he opened the cabin door and pulled Uncle Richard in after him.

As soon as the door was closed behind them,

Stephen said, "Uncle Richard, I'm not sure it was very cool to let her in on our secret. How can we trust her?"

"Don't worry," Uncle Richard said. "When you have as much experience as I've had, you'll know when to trust a woman. Besides, after that attempt on our lives this morning, we'll need all the help we can get."

Eight hours later Stephen was awakened by Uncle Richard's voice. "See, Steve, I told you we'd need help."

Stephen sat up in his bunk, rubbing his eyes.

"Take a look at this," said Uncle Richard. "There was a knock on the door. When I got up and opened it, no one was there. But there was this note shoved under the door."

Stephen looked at a note written in large, crude capital letters:

SOON YOU WILL LAND ON IONIA, HOME OF THE BURIED PALACE OF MINOS. IF YOU LOOK TOO CLOSELY AT WHAT IS GOING ON BENEATH THE SURFACE, YOU, TOO, WILL BE LOST FOR ALL TIME. IF YOU IGNORE THIS LETTER, IT WILL BE YOUR DEATH WARRANT.

7

TAKING THE PLUNGE

WEDNESDAY: 10:42 A.M.
Ionia

Professor Sophocles Democrites had snow-white hair, but his blue eyes gleamed with enthusiasm behind thick horn-rimmed glasses as he led Uncle Richard and Stephen on a tour of Ionia.

"When I first arrived here four years ago, this island was a deserted piece of rock. It supported no life other than nesting birds, lizards, and scorpions for over three thousand years—ever since the tidal wave from the volcanic explosion on Santorini swept Ionia clean not only of civilization but of vegetation," the professor said. "Now look at it."

Stephen and Uncle Richard looked around them at the small army of men working with everything from picks and shovels to pneumatic drills and bulldozers. They were uncovering the walls of a great Minoan palace.

"How did you pick this island to make your dig?" asked Uncle Richard.

"It was a gamble, the kind of gamble that an archaeologist must take," said the professor. "Five years ago a fisherman took refuge here from a sudden storm. After the storm he discovered an ancient ring on the shore. The ring was sent to Athens. It was about to be filed and forgotten in a museum basement as not important enough to be displayed when I saw it and recognized what it was."

"What was it?" asked Stephen. Archaeology seemed to offer mysteries as exciting as any that he and Uncle Richard had on their adventures.

The professor's face lit up at the memory.

"It was a Minoan seal ring. The key to solving the puzzle of where the people of Atlantis had taken their most valuable possessions when they fled that doomed island. This was where they landed, a place where they thought they would be safe. They could not dream that the same catastrophe that destroyed Santorini would reach them here—to kill them and to bury their treasure."

"Have you found it yet?" asked Stephen.

"Not yet, but soon, I'm sure," said the professor. "As you see, we have uncovered one of the largest Minoan palaces ever built." He pointed at the vast labyrinth of stone walls spreading before them, a structure that seemed the work of giants rather than ordinary human beings.

"Now all we have to do is discover the palace treasure vault. That's why I've just visited the palace of Knossos on Crete. It was the model for all other major Minoan palaces. I'll now correlate its dimensions with the dimensions of the palace here on Ionia to calculate where the treasure should be."

"Hey, maybe I can help you do that," said Stephen. He was thinking of his Kronom watch, and how easily its computing powers could solve the professor's problem. "I'm good with numbers. I got straight A's in math last year."

The professor smiled at him indulgently. "It's always refreshing to see the confidence and eagerness of the young."

"It might not be a bad idea to give Steve your numbers to play around with," said Uncle Richard, exchanging glances with Stephen. "He might surprise you."

"Of course I'll let him try to help me," said the professor. "Archaeology is always a team effort. And speaking of that, here comes a key member of our team now."

Stephen followed his gaze to see Midas, accompanied by Diana and Mr. Apollo, coming toward them. They moved at a slow pace, with Midas pausing every few steps to mop his dripping face.

"Ah, Midas, it's good to see you," said the professor. "I was just telling Mr. Duffy and his nephew what a key role you have played in this project. I can never repay my debt to you."

"Gads, sir, nonsense, you make me blush," said Midas, though his red face was the result of exertion rather than embarrassment. "It is I who owe you the debt, professor, for allowing me to participate in my small way in your great work."

"That goes double for me," said Mr. Apollo, pausing to touch the flame from a large gold lighter to the tip of a long cigar.

"But I do hope our visitors are having an interesting time here," said Diana, giving Uncle Richard a quick, meaningful glance.

"I assure you, we are," said Uncle Richard. "Of course, the really major discoveries are still below the surface, waiting to be brought to light."

"There's one thing you must see before you go any farther," said Midas. "The discovery with which the professor convinced me that he indeed was on the right track."

"Yes, you must see it," agreed the professor. "It was my first major find here, and it gave me the impetus to go on."

"And this is the perfect time to see it—as the heat of the day rises," Midas went on. "Indeed, I would enjoy going with you except that I would encounter

certain physical difficulties." He patted his huge stomach as if it were a pet dog.

"You see, it's thirty feet underwater," said the professor. "I found the remains of a fleet of Minoan ships, ships that could have carried thousands of people and their treasure to Ionia. The fleet must have been sunk in the harbor by the tidal wave, but there was only a scattering of valuables in the underwater wreckage. That could mean only that most of the treasure had been unloaded before the catastrophe struck."

"Can I go too?" said Stephen eagerly.

"I'm not sure how safe it would be," said Uncle Richard.

"But I'm good at scuba diving," Stephen said. "Remember that time we were underwater in Hawaii? I handled myself really well then."

"You must let the boy go, sir," said Midas heartily. "He has spirit, sir, real gumption. Come along with me. The scuba masks and air tanks are waiting. I can promise you an experience neither of you will ever forget. And I assure you there'll be no danger. You have my word on that."

Midas was right. It was an experience that Stephen would never forget, right from the moment he followed Uncle Richard off the yacht and into the water.

Below the surface was the most beautifully clear view he had ever imagined. It was like swimming down through pale green air.

Gradually the pale green grew darker as Stephen moved his legs in powerful frog kicks to keep pace with Uncle Richard, who was descending below him. A few moments later he caught up with Uncle Richard at the bottom of the harbor.

Uncle Richard was clinging to a piece of heavily rusted metal protruding from the sand. Stephen guessed that it must be the remains of a huge anchor.

Then he saw another piece of metal near Uncle Richard's and grabbed hold of it. Pressing a button on his waterproof Kronom K-D2, he sent forth a powerful beam of light. He played it over the harbor bottom.

He could see other pieces of metal sticking out of the sand. Thousands of years ago a great fleet of Minoan ships must have ridden at anchor here, before disaster destroyed them all.

Then Stephen saw something else—five scuba divers, knives in hand, swimming toward them.

Stephen looked at Uncle Richard, whose hand was reaching for his knife. But his fingers never reached the hilt.

Stephen saw a long tentacle snake around Uncle Richard's wrist while another wrapped around his ankle and still others circled his desperately writhing body.

From behind a large rock an octopus emerged to do battle with this invader of its territory.

Stephen watched horror-stricken as Uncle Richard

helplessly struggled to keep from being crushed to death.

At the same time the skin divers were moving in for the kill, their knives at the ready.

8

STEPHEN DOES A SOLO

WEDNESDAY: HIGH NOON
Ionia

Stephen did the only thing he could do.

He pulled out his own knife and propelled himself toward the octopus.

Fortunately, the octopus's last tentacle had just gone around Uncle Richard. Stephen was free to get near enough to the monstrous creature to strike his blade home in the one spot it would do any good.

Stephen summoned up all his strength and plunged the knife up to the hilt into the center of one of the octopus's protruding eyes.

The knife went in as easily as cutting through butter. Its tip must have reached the octopus's brain—because two things happened instantly.

The tentacles loosened around Uncle Richard. Then an inky black stream poured out of the octopus, turning into a billowing underwater cloud.

In the middle of the black cloud Stephen felt Uncle Richard's hand touch his arm. Stephen got the message as clearly as if he had heard it: Move it!

Side by side Uncle Richard and Stephen shot straight up through the water.

As they emerged from the blackness into the bright green water, Stephen was happy to find out that the scuba divers had vanished. Either they thought that the octopus was doing their dirty work for them or they'd lost sight of Uncle Richard and Stephen in the cloud of ink.

While treading water to catch their breath, Uncle Richard said between gasps, "Don't tell anyone we saw those scuba divers coming after us."

"I get it," said Stephen. "That way, whoever's after us will still think our guard is down."

"You're getting more savvy all the time," said Uncle Richard. "Pretty soon you'll be the one who tells me what to do in tight spots."

An hour later, aboard the yacht, Stephen did feel like telling Uncle Richard what to do—or rather, what not to do.

He wanted to tell Uncle Richard not to trust Diana Briggs so much, and not to let her so far into their plans.

Because that was exactly what Uncle Richard was

doing, ignoring the warning glances that Stephen kept throwing him.

As soon as Uncle Richard and Stephen were alone with Diana, Uncle Richard told her about their scuba divers.

"Who could have sent them after you?" she asked. "Whom do you suspect?"

"Anyone and everyone," said Uncle Richard. "Midas. Or Apollo. Or Stavros. I'm not even ruling out the professor. It wouldn't be the first time that a crook appeared to be the picture of respectability. Believe me, greed does strange things to the best of us."

"Not the *professor,*" Diana said. "I refuse to believe it." Then she paused. "Of course, he's always talking about how much money he needs for the work he loves so much. . . ."

"See what I mean?" said Uncle Richard. "Everyone has something he wants that money will help him get. And some people will stop at nothing for that money. Not even murder."

"Then perhaps you two shouldn't stay here," said Diana. "I mean, this really isn't your affair, and it does seem rather foolish to risk your lives to save a treasure that doesn't belong to you."

"I have a promise to keep to a friend," said Uncle Richard.

"Then at least let me help you," said Diana. "I owe you a favor for helping me out of that jam on the airplane, and your enemy or enemies would never suspect me."

"I was hoping you'd say that," said Uncle Richard. "And there is one thing you especially can do if both Stephen and I get in a jam."

"Uhh, Uncle Richard, maybe you and I should talk this—" said Stephen, trying to stop Uncle Richard before it was too late.

But Uncle Richard went on. "There's a miniaturized radio transmitter in our baggage. It's set on a special frequency that my friend Constantine is tuned into. If we call for help, he can helicopter in his men within a couple of hours."

"Well, that's good to know," said Diana. She laid her hand on Uncle Richard's arm and looked into his eyes. "I'm glad you told me. And not just because I can help you if you need me. It shows there's a real trust between us—and maybe something more. Something I could feel from the first moment we saw each other on the plane."

"Uhh, Uncle Richard," said Stephen, giving up hope of tearing his uncle away from his conversation with Diana. "I'm going off by myself. There's a couple of things I want to get done."

"Sure, see you later, Steve," said Uncle Richard, not taking his eyes off Diana.

Stephen left Uncle Richard and Diana standing with locked gazes. He went into his cabin and bolted the door. Then he took out the two maps that the professor had photocopied for him earlier that day.

One map was of the palace at Knossos on Crete. The other was of the palace the professor had unearthed on Ionia. The two palaces followed the same master plan. Only their sizes were different. It should have been easy for the professor to have figured out where the Ionian treasure vault was by comparing it to the location of the storerooms for valuables at Knossos. But so far the professor had failed.

Stephen might not have the professor's vast knowledge and experience, but he did have something that the professor did not have.

His Kronom K-D2

He fed the measurements of both palaces into the Kronom and programmed its computer to compare them and report whether anything was missing in the Ionian palace.

In two seconds the Kronom's voice readout replied: "Large room in southwest corner, and small stairway in northeast corner."

Stephen had suspected something like that. The professor's reconstruction of the Ionian palace was incomplete. He had missed some fragments of walls scattered by the tidal wave or worn to dust by time.

Using voice control, Stephen commanded: "Make map of palace with missing room and stairway restored. Then locate treasure vault based on Knossos model. Use X to mark the spot."

Instantly a revised map appeared on the watch display screen. Turning out the light in the cabin, Stephen pressed a button and aimed the screen at a large piece of photographic paper. The Kronom printed an enlarged map on the paper.

Stephen inspected the new map. The X was a full hundred yards from where the professor had made his latest dig. Stephen knew that in time the professor would have corrected his error by himself, but Stephen felt the glow of pleasure at doing it first.

He also had a question to ask himself.

Should he tell the professor—after Uncle Richard had said that no one could be trusted?

Uncle Richard was right. Stephen couldn't trust anyone. He couldn't even trust Uncle Richard not to spill the beans to Diana.

Stephen could trust only himself.

He would find out if the Kronom was right.

The more he thought about the idea, the better he liked it. He could see why people became dedicated archaeologists—to know the thrill of being the first to shed light on the treasures of the past.

He could hardly wait. Unfortunately, he did have to wait until one o'clock in the afternoon of the next day, when as usual the sun beat down like a white hot hammer.

Not even the professor's eagerness to press forward with the dig could make the workmen give up their three-hour break for eating and drinking, then taking a nap in their tents.

The excavation site was deserted as Stephen moved through the complex labyrinth of walls and trenches, checking his map as he walked.

He found the spot he was looking for. He saw that a hole had already been started there. It had gone down over nine feet without uncovering anything.

Stephen checked his map again.

This *had* to be the spot.

The Kronom was *never* wrong.

Or was it?

There was one way to find out. Stephen lowered a nearby ladder into the hole and grabbed a pick and shovel. He dropped the tools into the hole ahead of him, then climbed down the ladder.

The hole was dark and cool, and the earth at the bottom was soft. It was easy going as he dug—until voices from above stopped him in mid-stroke.

The first voice was Diana's.

"Then the big move is set for tonight," she said. "But you remember what you promised me."

The second voice was Midas's.

"Diana, my dear, your suspicion cuts me to the quick. Of course I will keep my promise. You'll get your full share—and a bonus for your latest contribution. It's extremely valuable to know who Richard Duffy is. Before, I was merely trying to scare him and his nephew off. Now I will have to take sterner methods."

"Just remember your promise," said Diana.

"Of course I will," said Midas. "But you must agree, all obstacles to our success must be removed as soon as possible."

"Like now?" Diana laughed.

Stephen tensed. There was no cheer in that laugh.

Terror ran like an electric shock through him as clods of earth started showering down.

Dirt was falling into his mouth as he opened it to shout for help.

But even as he began to scream he knew there was no one to hear him.

Except the two people who were burying him alive!

9

TREASURE!

THURSDAY: 1:39 P.M.
Ionia

Even as Stephen shouted he realized that he was falling. The earth beneath his feet was giving way.

He landed feetfirst on what felt like a pile of loose rubble and lost his balance. He steadied himself, and shined the light from his Kronom downward.

He was standing on top of a huge clay pot, taller than he was. The lid was off, and his feet were resting on the objects filling the pot to its rim. He shined the light on them and saw the gleam of gold and the dazzling glitter of jewels. Then he played the light around the underground chamber. It was filled with other huge, elaborately decorated pots.

"I've done it! I've found the treasure!" he shouted at the top of his lungs.

Only when he heard his voice echoing upward did he realize his mistake.

Midas and Diana must have heard him. And now only he stood between them and the treasure they hungered for.

He drew in his breath, as if trying to take back his shout.

Then he let out his breath as he heard Uncle Richard's voice from above. "Hold on, Steve! We're getting a ladder down to you!"

Minutes later Stephen was standing blinking in the near-blinding sunlight. Clustered around him were Uncle Richard, Midas, Diana, the professor, and a group of sleepy-looking workmen.

"I say, a bit of luck we happened to be passing by," said Diana. "I was taking Midas to see some interesting frescos we uncovered this morning. Suddenly we heard your voice."

"Some coincidence," said Stephen.

Before Stephen could say more, Uncle Richard said, "It's even more of a coincidence that I was taking the professor to this very spot. When we arrived we saw Diana and Midas, and then we heard your shout."

"Mr. Duffy was kind enough to come to me at noontime and offer his own calculations on where the treasure room was," said the professor. Uncle Richard winked at Stephen and tapped his Kronom.

"I'd arrived at the same conclusion as Mr. Duffy

this morning,'' the professor went on. ''But I wanted some time to double-check my figures, since I have been so disappointed by my miscalculations in the past. But when Mr. Duffy's findings matched mine, I saw no reason to wait any longer. We woke up a work party and came here at once. But. congratulations, young man. You beat us to it.''

''It was really nothing,'' said Stephen, feeling the flush of pride mingled with embarrassment.

''Gads, my boy, don't be so modest,'' said Midas. ''Let me be the first to shake your hand.'' And he extended a huge, fat hand that felt to Stephen like a slab of raw fish steak.

''And now,'' said Midas, ''let's see what we've found.''

By sunset that evening a vast collection of gold coins and ornaments, jewels and Minoan religious objects stood in front of the tent that served as the professor's headquarters on the island.

Stephen, though, was too impatient to enjoy this feast for the eyes. He had to tell Uncle Richard about the conversation he had overheard between Diana and Midas.

Finally Stephen succeeded in drawing Uncle Richard off to one side while the others were gaping at the treasure. But before Stephen could say anything, Diana herself came over to join them.

''I know what you're about to say to your uncle,'' she said. ''And I want to explain what I'm sure you must have overheard. You see, it was the only way I could think of to find out if Midas was as honest as he claimed. As soon as the professor confided to me that he thought he had found the treasure spot, I told Midas about it. I pretended to be willing to betray both you and the professor, and Midas took me up on it. He let me in on his plan."

"What is his plan?" asked Uncle Richard, his steely gray eyes suddenly hard and alert.

"He planned to beat the professor to the treasure," said Diana. "Midas and his men would carry it off during the night. When the professor dug tomorrow, he'd find the treasure chamber empty. He'd be left thinking he had made yet another miscalculation—or that his entire theory about the lost treasure was a mistake."

"Well, we wrecked that plan," said Stephen.

"You certainly did," said Diana, giving Stephen a smile that gave him an idea of the effect she had on Uncle Richard.

"Maybe Midas will now abandon his schemes," Diana went on. "The professor is too famous for even Midas to trifle with."

"I wouldn't count on that," said Uncle Richard. "I took a good look at Midas as the treasure piled up in front of his eyes. He looked like a child with his face pressed against a candy-store window. And unfortunately, Midas has the tools to break the glass and grab the goodies. I'm talking about his hired help—Apollo, Stavros, and probably the whole army of diggers that Stavros commands."

"Fortunately, he also has me. At least he *thinks* he does," said Diana. "I'll be able to give you advance word on his plans. I can tell the professor too, though I hope I don't have to. I wouldn't want to disrupt his work by worrying him unless it was absolutely necessary. Anyway, you'll all be safe. Forewarned is forearmed. And I'll be your weapon."

"Speaking of weapons," said Uncle Richard, "look at the one that the professor has."

The professor was walking toward them with an ax almost five feet long. The head had a cutting edge on both sides, and it was made of solid gold.

"I know you'll want to see this," said the professor when he reached Uncle Richard, Stephen, and Diana. Close at his heels were Midas, Apollo, and Stavros, like wolves who had scented prey.

"The workmen have just brought this to the surface. It is the most magnificent discovery of my entire career—and one of the greatest archaeological finds of all time. This is the sacred double-headed ax of the Minoans, used to make animal sacrifices to their mother goddess. There have been others like it found, but none as big and beautifully preserved as this one."

"Gads, sir," said Midas, his eyes gleaming as brightly as the golden ax, "this is a moment I will never forget. To have been of aid in recovering this marvelous legacy of the human spirit and of human skill—I tell you I am simply overwhelmed with joy and modest pride. And I am sure I speak also for Mr. Apollo."

"Yeah, right," said Apollo, not taking his eyes from the ax for a second.

Stephen and Uncle Richard exchanged glances. Any doubts about the intentions of Midas and his men were gone now.

The only question was: How, when, and where would they make their move?

Uncle Richard looked at Diana, and she caught his message. She nodded almost imperceptibly.

"But now let us celebrate," Midas said. "I have a wine I purchased months ago especially for this occasion. A rare and delicious vintage made on the island of Santorini. I thought it only fitting that we enjoy this modern treasure of Atlantis to celebrate our discovery of the ancient one. And it is only fitting that you, Professor, enjoy the first triumphant taste."

Midas snapped his fingers, and a crewman came up bearing one of the large golden, jeweled goblets that had just been unearthed. Midas had had it cleaned and filled with the golden wine. He took it from the crewman and handed it to the professor.

"You'll find it deliciously rich and sweet," said Midas, "as rich and sweet as this discovery is for all of us."

The professor raised the goblet to his lips. Then he lowered it.

"But I insist you all join me," he said.

"Later, sir, later," said Midas. "I want you to have this one moment of glory alone. Please, allow me this little whim."

"Of course," said the professor. "I owe you this much at least—and so much more. I only wish I could give you the reward you deserve."

"Gads, sir, don't worry about that," said Midas, watching the professor take a deep drink of the wine. "I assure you, my reward is coming."

"You were right, this wine is simply delicious. Let me again thank—" the professor began, then stopped abruptly. A puzzled look came over his face. The goblet slipped from his fingers and fell to the ground. The professor tottered and began to fall. The crewman caught him and lowered him gently to the ground.

"What the—" said Uncle Richard, starting to move forward. He was stopped by the revolvers suddenly in the hands of Midas, Apollo, and Stavros.

"I was hoping this unpleasant confrontation could be avoided, believe me, sir," said Midas with a sad shrug of his shoulders. "But you simply would not take my gentle hints to go away, and now I'm afraid it is too late to let you. The only question now is, what will be the best way to make you disappear permanently. It is a matter that deserves careful consideration. I believe I will sleep on it. You and your nephew should thank me for that, sir. It gives you one more full night to enjoy being alive."

Then he ordered his men, "Tie them up—and make sure they cannot escape!"

10

INTO THE LABYRINTH

THURSDAY: MIDNIGHT
Ionia

This was not the way Stephen would have chosen to spend his last night on earth.

He had lain on the dirt floor of a small tent for hours, bound hand and foot with heavy, rough hemp that tore at his skin when he tried to wriggle out of it.

Four feet away Uncle Richard lay in the same position.

The tent entrance flap was open. Full moonlight poured through it, showing a guard sitting in the entrance with a rifle cradled in his arms.

Stephen heard a dull, clunking sound. The rifle had slipped from the guard's arms, and his head dropped forward. He had fallen asleep.

But it didn't matter. Stephen strained at the ropes around him. They held firm.

Then, suddenly, he felt the ropes being untied.

Uncle Richard, silent as a cat, had somehow freed himself and come to Stephen's aid.

"How did you get loose?" Stephen whispered after Uncle Richard had put the guard into an even deeper sleep with an expertly directed karate chop, then bound and gagged him.

"A little trick an Indian *fakir* in Calcutta showed me," said Uncle Richard. "You expand your muscles when you're being tied up, then contract them when you want to get free. I've been able to slip out of those ropes for hours, but I had to wait until the guard wasn't watching."

"You think you could show me how to do it sometime?" said Stephen.

"Sometime, but not now," said Uncle Richard. "We have things to do. Move it!"

With Uncle Richard leading the way they moved cautiously out of the tent. It was on the edge of the cluster of tents that housed the workers. Those tents, and the professor's tent two hundred yards away, with the treasure still piled up in front of it, and the palace ruins beyond all formed a silent landscape bathed in silver moonlight.

"First we have to find the professor and make sure he's still alive," said Uncle Richard. "Who knows what Midas put in that wine."

"And then we have to make sure Diana is safe," said Stephen. "You know, I feel like apologizing to her. I actually suspected her of being on the other side. I didn't realize she was the best friend we had."

"First let's worry about the professor," said Uncle Richard.

"Right," said Stephen. "Diana's one lady who knows how to look after herself."

"No argument there," said Uncle Richard, moving toward the professor's tent. "I hope they haven't taken him out to the yacht already."

Then Uncle Richard said, "Uh-oh, bad news. There's no guard. They must have taken him. Come on, let's check."

They approached the professor's tent from the rear, then Uncle Richard went around the tent in one direction, and Stephen in the other. They met on opposite sides of the tent entrance. Stephen followed Uncle Richard's lead in moving his head forward just enough to peek inside.

There was no one inside except a figure lying on a camp bed illuminated by a beam of moonlight.

Uncle Richard gestured, and they both entered the tent.

The professor was lying there absolutely still. Quickly Uncle Richard checked his pulse.

"He's still alive," said Uncle Richard with relief.

"But whatever they gave him must have knocked him out for a long time."

At that moment both Uncle Richard and Stephen heard voices and footsteps outside. The two of them darted into a shadowed corner of the tent just as Midas, Apollo, Stavros, and four burly crewmen came in.

Midas walked up to the professor and looked down at him.

"Good, that drug lived up to its reputation. The professor will remain out of the picture for another day at least."

"Yes, and we can give him another dose when this one wears off," said Apollo.

"Why don't we just knock him off and get it over with?" asked Stavros. "We got what we came for. Now we just have to get rid of anyone who might squeal."

"Gentlemen, gentlemen," said Midas, shaking his head, "let us not be so crude. We don't have to kill the professor. I have a solution that will solve all our problems. As they say in chess, it is an elegant solution."

"Yeah? Let us in on it," said Stavros.

"It better be good," said Apollo. "Stavros and I both must agree on it. Remember, without my underworld connections and Stavros's hired muscle, you can do nothing."

"My good fellow, I assure you my plan is good,

very good,'' said Midas. ''You'll love it when you hear it.''

Stephen wanted to make sure he heard it too. He edged a step closer, and the side of his foot brushed against something solid.

He moved back. Too late.

A stack of books piled on the floor toppled over with a loud crash.

''Move it!'' yelled Uncle Richard.

Stephen matched Uncle Richard stride for stride as they dashed for the tent entrance, right past Midas and the others.

They had barely made it outside when Midas shouted, ''After them! Wake up the whole crew! Don't let them escape!''

Midas didn't have to worry, Stephen thought. Even as he ran, Stephen knew there was no escape from this tiny island. All it offered was a perfect place to hide.

And Uncle Richard was heading for it, racing a few steps ahead of Stephen through the moonlight that lit the island.

The palace ruins.

The Minoans had built their palaces in a series of complex passageways and staircases that had been the origin of the legend of the labyrinth, in which men could lose their way forever.

They had reached that labyrinth now.

"This way!" Uncle Richard half-whispered over his shoulder as he darted into a passageway.

A few minutes later they were deep inside the labyrinth. They paused, catching their breath, until they heard the sound of running footsteps and shouting voices, and saw the glow of approaching flashlights.

Again Uncle Richard and Stephen started running, going around a turn and up stone steps to another level of the palace. There they paused once more. This time it took even less time for their pursuers to get too close for comfort. From the noise, it was obvious that many more of them had joined the hunt.

"Just when I almost had it," said Uncle Richard angrily.

"Had what?" asked Stephen.

"Constantine's high secret radio frequency," said Uncle Richard. "The radio he gave us is automatically beamed in on it, but there's a few hundred thousand combinations that my Kronom has to check—and there wasn't enough time. Maybe later. Move it!"

Uncle Richard was off and running again—even faster than before. Stephen followed after him and stumbled over a loose rock.

He managed not to fall. But in the few seconds it took him to regain his balance, Uncle Richard had vanished from view.

Stephen let out all the stops as he tore off in the direction where Uncle Richard had disappeared, then came to a dead halt.

In front of him the passageway divided.

Which branch had Uncle Richard taken?

There wasn't time to think. Stephen chose the left branch and hoped he was correct.

He dashed along the passageway. Ahead of him he saw only blackness. Then, as he rounded a sharp turn, he saw a rectangle of moonlight where the passage ended.

Suddenly a figure appeared in the moonlight, and Stephen froze, pressing against the rough stone wall.

The figure definitely wasn't Uncle Richard.

It was Diana Briggs.

She must have fled into the labyrinth, too, to hide out until help came.

Maybe she had even managed to get off a radio signal to Constantine, since Uncle Richard had been smart enough to tell her about the radio and where it was hidden in their luggage.

He'd find out soon enough.

"Diana!" he whispered as loudly as he dared. "Don't be frightened. It's me. Steve."

She stepped into the passageway toward him, and he moved to meet her.

Suddenly he felt her hands grab his arms with a strength he had not imagined she possessed.

Her voice was stronger than he imagined it could be too. Then she shouted, "I've caught the boy! Come help me hold him!"

11

DEN OF THIEVES

FRIDAY: 1:32 A.M.
Ionia

Two workmen came running to Diana's aid. They took hold of Stephen. Their calloused hands felt like vises on his arms.

A moment later Apollo and Stavros arrived. Close on their heels came Midas, panting.

"Now we just got to get the uncle," said Stavros.

"That'll be easy," said Apollo. He pulled out a large automatic pistol and pressed the muzzle against the side of Stephen's head.

"Hey, Duffy!" Apollo called out into the darkness. "Give yourself up or I blow the kid's head off! Don't think I'm playing games! I've done a lot worse stuff, believe me!"

"I believe you," said Uncle Richard, stepping out of the darkness less than ten feet away.

"I doubled back on my trail when I realized I had lost you," Uncle Richard said to Stephen. "But I couldn't get to you in time."

"You should be happy then, sir," said Midas. "You and your nephew are together now. You will have the pleasure of sharing the same fate. We'll go to the yacht now, where we will decide it."

"Remember your promise," said Diana.

"And which promise was that, my dear?" said Midas.

"That nobody would be killed," said Diana.

"Oh, *that* promise," said Midas. "I'm so sorry, but it is difficult to keep my promises straight. It seems I made so many of them."

"Yeah, you sure did," said Apollo. "And it's time to make good on the big ones you made—to *us*." He gestured toward Stavros and the men standing around him.

"Promises, promises," said Midas, shaking his head as if weary with an unpleasant burden. "Back to the yacht, then, where we can select the ones that are worth keeping."

Back in the main cabin of the yacht, Uncle Richard and Stephen were forced to sit down, then tied to chairs placed against the wall. The crewmen were ordered to leave, while Midas, Diana, Apollo, and Stavros sat at a large round table under a bright overhead light in the center of the cabin. As Stephen watched and listened to them he felt as if he were witnessing a poker game being played with words rather than cards. The stakes were high—a fortune in treasure and his and Uncle Richard's lives.

"I figure we made ourselves a nice profit," said Apollo. "The cost of the operation, counting labor, materials, and the rest, was maybe a million. And when we melt down the gold and separate the jewels, we'll have valuables we can sell for seven million, even if we have to take a discount from market prices. I've got to admit, Midas, when this thing dragged on for a whole year I was becoming dubious, but it was worth it."

Midas allowed himself a deep, rumbling chuckle before he replied. "Gads, sir, you have no idea of the fortune we have in our grasp," he said. "Melt down the gold and separate the jewels indeed! Don't you see, the value of this treasure lies in its historical and artistic importance. When I dispose of it in the world underground art market, the take will be closer to forty million than seven. Of course, it will take a certain amount of time and delicacy to negotiate."

"How *much* time?" asked Stavros.

"Two years, perhaps three," said Midas, shifting his huge bulk in his chair as if he had suddenly felt an unexpected twinge. "In these matters it is hard to give a precise timetable. But I assure you—"

"And just who is going to conduct these negotiations?'' Apollo interrupted in a voice as sharp and hard as his gaze.

''Why myself, of course,'' said Midas. ''Who else has the connections with the great secret collectors of the world, from international billionaires to some of the most famous names in entertainment? All I ask is that you trust me, and you will be rewarded beyond your wildest dreams of wealth.''

Midas paused to hear the dead silence that greeted his words. He cleared his throat. ''Gentlemen, gentlemen, you must realize my word is my bond. Ask anyone who—''

''Yeah, sure we trust you,'' said Apollo. ''But let's make this little discussion nice and democratic. I say we vote on it, the three of us. The girl doesn't count. She didn't put up any dough. She's just part of the hired help.''

''You mean *those* two are backing this too?'' Diana said to Midas. ''I thought that only you were. That's what you told me.''

''My dear girl,'' said Midas with an apologetic shrug. ''I didn't want to bother your lovely head with sordid business matters.''

''Enough talk. Time to vote,'' said Apollo. ''First, those in favor of melting down the gold and separating and selling the jewels. Here's my vote.'' Apollo pulled out his pistol and laid it on the table with the barrel pointed directly at Midas.

"And here's mine," said Stavros, pulling out his pistol and doing the same.

"Gentlemen, in the land where democracy was invented, I will not argue with such clear evidence of the will of the majority," said Midas. "Seven million dollars may not be the same as forty million, but it is far better than nothing."

"But you *can't* let them melt down the treasure," said Diana, her face growing pale. "This is one of the greatest archaeological finds in history. It can't be lost again, and this time for ever."

"Let us merely pretend it was never found, my dear," said Midas. "You should be able to do that. You have proven yourself to be so very good at pretending."

"Yes, I have been good at pretending," said Diana, her voice dropping. "Even to myself."

"Forget the girl," said Apollo. "She's got to go along with us. She's in too deep to pull out. Let's just finish up this business and get off this island. I want to see some bright lights again, and start enjoying some of the gains."

"Yeah, we just knock off the professor, this American snoop, and the kid—and we're home free," said Stavros.

"Midas, you promised at the very start that the professor wouldn't be harmed in any way," said Diana. "That's one promise I insist you keep."

"My dear, what sort of scoundrel do you think I

am?'' said Midas. ''Rest assured, the professor will not be harmed.''

''We can't let him live—he knows too much,'' said Stavros, his hand closing over his gun.

Apollo gripped his gun as well.

''Gentlemen, gentlemen,'' Midas said. ''Let us not be hasty. Our safe and secure future depends on careful planning now. We do not want to have to explain the disappearance of the professor. Nor does the professor have to disappear. After all, what does the professor know?''

''Plenty,'' said Apollo. ''He knows we found the treasure.''

''But let me remind you, *he will not know what happened to it,*'' said Midas. ''Remember, the professor is unconscious now, and will stay that way for as long as we wish. When we finally let him wake he will find that the treasure has disappeared—*along with the yacht and the two Americans here.*''

Stephen, listening, felt his stomach turn over. He realized what Midas meant.

Stephen looked at Uncle Richard and saw his jaw tightening. Uncle Richard knew too.

Diana did as well. Her mouth opened in shock.

It took a few seconds for Apollo to get the idea. His face lit with an ugly smile. ''Hey, pretty good,'' he said.

Stavros's face stayed blank. ''I don't get it,'' he said.

"My plan, sir, is beautiful in its simplicity, a work of art, if I may say so," said Midas. "We will simply cause the Americans and the yacht to vanish at the same time, and ship the treasure back to Athens in the trawler we have waiting a few miles offshore. When the professor wakes up we will tell him that the Americans disappeared with the yacht and the treasure after putting all of us to sleep. We will even be paid for losing the yacht. We have an excellent insurance policy."

"But you're talking about murder," said Diana.

"It is either them or your respected professor, my dear," said Midas. "What else would you have us do?"

Diana turned and looked at Uncle Richard and Stephen.

"Believe me, I'm sorry," she said. "But the professor is one of the greatest scholars in the world, and I am an archaeologist first."

"Don't worry, my dear," said Midas, patting her shoulder. "You'll be able to drown your sorrow in champagne from now on. This regrettable incident will soon be forgotten, as forgotten as the treasure of Atlantis was for so long, and now will be again."

"Enough talk," said Apollo, picking up his pistol. "Let's get the show on the road."

Stavros picked up his pistol, too, then shouted out a command in Greek. Four crewmen entered the cabin, untied Uncle Richard and Stephen, and jerked them to their feet.

As Uncle Richard and Stephen were hustled down the corridor to their cabin, Uncle Richard managed to catch Stephen's eye. He gave Stephen a quick wink. Stephen knew what that meant.

Uncle Richard had a plan.

Stephen hoped it would work. It had better.

Their cabin door was open and Uncle Richard and Stephen were roughly thrown inside. Stavros was about to slam the door and lock it when one of the crewmen pointed to Uncle Richard and said something in Greek.

Stavros gave a wolfish grin and nodded.

As Stavros and Apollo trained their pistols on Uncle Richard and Stephen, the crewman entered the cabin and held out his hand.

"He wants your watches," said Apollo. "They caught his eye. Give them to him, and fast. And don't feel bad about it. You're not going to need them ever again."

Desperately Stephen looked at Uncle Richard to see what to do.

Uncle Richard was looking at the guns. He unbuckled his Kronom and handed it over. Stephen had no choice but to do the same. As soon as the Kronom was off his wrist he felt more naked and defenseless than he had ever felt on any of his adventures with Uncle Richard.

Pleased with his pretty new watches, the crewman asked Stavros a question in Greek.

"He wants to know if you can do things with them, like set an alarm and stuff like that," Stavros said.

"Sure you can," said Uncle Richard. "They're the best Japanese watches that $19.95 can buy." Satisfied, the crewman and Stavros left.

As soon as the door was slammed and locked, Stephen turned to Uncle Richard.

"What's your plan?" he asked. "We don't have much time."

Uncle Richard looked at his naked wrist.

"My plan just went out that door," he said.

12

OUT OF THE FRYING PAN

FRIDAY: 4:39 A.M.
Ionia

Stephen and Uncle Richard stared helplessly at each other.

Stephen was the first to speak.

"I've got a plan!" he said.

"Good work," said Uncle Richard. "Because this is one time in my life I've run out of plans."

"There's one thing we completely forgot," said Stephen. "The radio that Constantine gave us. It's still in our luggage. We can call Constantine and he can helicopter help to us. It might take Midas and the others a while to figure out how to destroy this yacht. Constantine might get here in time. It's our only chance."

Before Stephen spoke, Uncle Richard's expression had been eager with anticipation. Now it once again grew dim with dejection.

"Great plan, Steve," he said. "The trouble is, it won't work."

"What won't work?" asked Stephen.

"The radio won't work," said Uncle Richard. "I already tried it just a few hours ago, to check it out. Somebody sabotaged it."

"Diana!" said Stephen.

"Nobody else," agreed Uncle Richard.

"I knew you never should have trusted her," said Stephen.

"I never did," said Uncle Richard. "I wanted her to *think* we trusted her, so that she and the rest of the gang would believe they had us under control and wouldn't worry about us. I told her about the radio just so she could wreck it and think we were defenseless. I figured I could use the Kronom to radio Constantine just as I could have used the Kronom to pick the lock on the cabin door. Looks like I figured wrong."

"But there must be *some* way to get out of here," said Stephen. "There always is."

"There always has been in the past," said Uncle Richard.

But after a feverish hour of checking out every inch of the locked door, the thick, unbreakable locked portholes, the solid walls, floor, and ceiling, Uncle

Richard stopped and said, "No way. There's nothing to do but wait and find out how they plan to destroy the yacht and us. I wonder how they'll do it."

As if in answer to his question, they heard a crash. Stephen stiffened. There was another crash, and both Stephen and Uncle Richard turned toward the door.

A few crashes later a crack appeared in the door, and soon after that, a piece of wood fell away to reveal a flash of golden metal.

It was the golden double-headed ax of the Minoans.

Furiously swinging it was Diana.

"It was the only tool I could find," she explained after she had made a hole large enough to enter through.

"What are you doing here?" asked Uncle Richard.

"I'm getting you out of here," she said, "before this whole yacht is blown to kingdom come. Which should be in a few minutes now."

"But *why*?" asked Stephen.

"Let's just say I've changed my mind," said Diana. "But there's no time for chitchat."

"Right," said Uncle Richard. "Move it!"

"Grab the radio," said Diana. "I've still got the part I took out of it. We can make it work once we get ashore."

As they climbed the stairs to the deck Diana said, "Keep low when you get on deck. They're watching from the shore. It was dark when I got here, but it's getting brighter now. I've tied the motor launch I

used to get here to the seaward side of the yacht where they can't see it—I hope.''

They clambered down the rope ladder that Diana had hooked into the yacht railing from the launch. She tossed the golden ax into the stern, gunned the engine, and headed out to sea.

''I'll head seaward until we're out of sight, then circle around and land on the other side of the island,'' she said. ''I've got the missing radio part there, and some guns I lifted from Midas's arsenal. We can radio your friend and then take care of ourselves until he arrives.''

''It's good to have you on our side,'' said Uncle Richard. ''I knew you wouldn't let them kill us if you could help it.''

''Let's say I wouldn't have *liked* them to kill you,'' said Diana. ''What I couldn't *stand* was the idea of their melting down all those irreplaceable relics. I wouldn't have minded the pieces going into private collections where they would have been discovered in fifty or a hundred years. But I didn't want them lost forever. As I said, I'm an archaeologist first.''

''Whatever you say, we owe you a lot—our lives,'' said Uncle Richard.

''I hope you remember that when the time comes to help me,'' said Diana.

''Don't worry,'' said Uncle Richard. ''You can trust me.''

"That's what Midas said when he made me all those pretty promises of lots of lovely money with nothing ugly involved," said Diana. She glanced at her watch, and said, "Look at the yacht, and brace yourself!"

Stephen and Uncle Richard looked back just in time to see a huge explosion tear off the prow of the yacht. Another explosion ripped up its deck. And then another, far larger than the first two combined, sent the entire vessel up in bits of shattered wood and metal and canvas.

A wave set from the explosion smashed into the motor launch, making it rock like a cradle out of control. When Stephen looked for the yacht again, after fighting to keep from being swept off the launch by the wash of water, he saw nothing but an unbroken expanse of sea.

"If Uncle Richard doesn't remember what we owe you," he promised Diana, "I'll remind him."

"Let's worry about that later," said Uncle Richard, looking away from where the yacht had been and toward the island, small now in the distance. "We're not out of this jam yet. Move it before they spot us."

Diana pulled back the throttle all the way, and the launch headed farther out to sea. Then she swung the craft around in a wide circle. An hour later the launch entered a small cove on the opposite side of the island. Twenty feet from land she cut the engine and let the launch drift the rest of the way to beach itself on a narrow strip of fine white sand at the head of the cove.

"What a beautiful spot," she said as they stood on the beach.

Stephen could see what she meant—the sea, the sky, the foliage by the shore, and the rocky highlands sprinkled with trees and bright flowers in the island's center.

"Too bad human beings had to spoil it," said Uncle Richard. "Where did you store the weapons and the radio part?"

"In a cave just up the hill," said Diana. "I discovered it in the first explorations of the island with the professor four years ago. It's a perfect hiding place."

She led the way up a hill to a narrow opening between two large boulders almost entirely concealed by foliage. Taking out a flashlight, she led them into a large, damp cavern that sloped down, taking them far beneath the surface. Daggerlike stalactites hung from the ceiling, and the liquid that had formed them over thousands of years still dripped downward from their sharp tips like pale blood.

"Nice place to visit, but I wouldn't want to live here," said Uncle Richard.

"Or die here," said Stephen, shivering despite himself.

"Welcome to my parlor, said the spider to the fly," boomed out a voice that echoed through the recesses of the cavern.

Diana, Uncle Richard, and Stephen froze.

"Gads, I don't mind telling you, you three have proved most troublesome," the voice went on. "You have destroyed my faith in human honesty and straightforward dealings forever. And now I'm afraid you must pay the penalty."

There was no mistaking who was speaking now. Midas. Or where the voice came from. The cave mouth, far above them.

"Quick, where are the weapons?" whispered Uncle Richard. "We'll have to try to shoot our way out. I can lay down covering fire to move them away from the entrance, and you can make a break for it."

Diana pointed to bundles of waterproof canvas lying by a cave wall. Swiftly Uncle Richard unwrapped two pistols and a submachine gun. He handed the pistols to Stephen and Diana, took the submachine gun for himself, and gestured for them to follow him slowly and cautiously up toward the cave entrance.

They were five feet away when the figure of Midas appeared in the cave mouth to block off the light.

"Freeze!" said Uncle Richard. "We've got three guns on you."

"Gads, sir, you should speak more gently," said Midas. "You almost frightened me to death."

"I'm going to do more than frighten you if you don't cooperate," said Uncle Richard.

"You mean you'd actually shoot me in cold blood,"

said Midas. "I'm shocked, sir, truly shocked. But if you feel you have to kill me, please go ahead. Pull the trigger. Don't let me stand in your way."

A shadow of doubt passed over Uncle Richard's face. Pointing his weapon toward the ground, he pulled the trigger. Nothing happened.

"I must apologize, sir, for leading you on," said Midas. "I should have mentioned that those weapons we allowed Miss Briggs to purloin had their firing pins removed. We merely wanted to find out how far she could be trusted, and I'm afraid we found out. I must say, I was grievously disappointed, though I can't say that Mr. Apollo and Mr. Stavros were. They are only too happy to have one less person to share the treasure with."

Apollo's angry voice cut in from behind Midas. "Come on, let's finish up with them and start loading the treasure on the trawler."

"Again I am forced to bow to the majority rule of my partners," said Midas. "I must bid you a hasty farewell. In a moment a boulder will be rolled over the mouth of this cave—and then another. I'm sure you'd be able to remove them in a year or two of digging, but somehow I don't think you'll survive that long without food, water, or air. Perhaps in a few hundred years archaeologists will discover your remains and have a simply fascinating mystery on their hands."

Stephen could already hear sounds of workmen rolling a boulder toward the cave entrance.

Midas, though, had one more thing to say before he stepped aside. "To spare you further wasted effort," he said, "you needn't bother trying to use the radio you brought with you. You'll find that more than the part that Miss Briggs removed is now missing."

Then Midas was gone, and in his place was a rock, the color of a tombstone.

At that moment the light from Diana's flashlight began to flicker.

"I knew I should have changed the battery," she said.

Then, pitch darkness.

The darkness of the grave.

13

BACKS TO THE WALL

FRIDAY: 11:30 A.M.
Ionia

"They must have followed me when I hid the weapons in the cave," said Diana's voice in the darkness. "I merely led you from one trap into another. I'm sorry."

After that there was only silence, a silence so intense that Stephen could almost hear the beating of his own heart.

Then he heard something else: the sound of the boulder being rolled away.

And then he was blinded by a patch of light where the boulder had been.

"Someone's come to rescue us," said Stephen.

"Don't get your hopes up," said Uncle Richard. "I was wondering if they'd remember we have the golden ax with us. They did, and they're coming back for it. Still, it gives us one more chance. Maybe I can jump them. Get ready."

But none of them were ready for the voice that called into the cave.

"Come out with your hands up."

Stephen tried to place the voice, but he couldn't, even when it continued. "And bring the sacred double-headed ax with you."

Only when they emerged into the sunlight, with Uncle Richard holding the ax high in one hand, could Stephen identify the man who had rescued them.

He was the man they last had seen being led away by the police in the Iraklion airport.

The tall, red-haired skyjacker.

The leader of HATE.

Zeus.

With him were at least twenty heavily armed men.

Facing their guns were Midas, Apollo, Stavros, and a group of workmen, all with hands held high.

"You see, sir, they do have the ax," Midas said. "As I told you, they are the thieves of your noble art treasures. We caught them red-handed with the ax and imprisoned them in the cave until we could notify the proper authorities."

"So we meet again," said Zeus to Uncle Richard. "I daresay you are surprised to see me. That is because you do not realize how widespread our movement is. Even in prison I found supporters to help me escape. And there were others in Iraklion to tell me of the expedition to this island. I have come here with my men to show all the world what we will do to those who seek to steal our ancient heritage."

"Gads, what a noble cause," said Midas. "Let me be the first to congratulate you on capturing these criminals. Believe me, sir, I will fully support any punishment you choose to deal out to them."

"Don't let him fool you," said Uncle Richard. "They're the ones who are the thieves. We tried to stop them. You came just in the nick of time. Ask him what his trawler is doing offshore, ready to take his loot away."

"Don't believe him," said Midas.

"Don't believe *him*," said Uncle Richard.

"I don't believe either of you," said Zeus. "You are all thieves, fighting for the spoils of your crime. And you will share the same punishment—a punishment that will make sure that no one will ever want to steal Greek art treasures again."

"I'll return one art treasure to you now," said Uncle Richard. "Here, catch!"

He tossed the golden ax in a high arc toward the HATE leader. All eyes turned upward to follow its flight. Zeus's hands went up to catch the ax and Uncle Richard dived for his knees before any of the terrorists' guns could be trained low enough to stop him.

The leader went down with Uncle Richard. Then

Uncle Richard rose and lifted Zeus up, holding him like a shield in front of him with an arm hooked around the leader's throat.

"One false move from any of you and I snap his neck like a twig," Uncle Richard told the gunmen as their fingers twitched on their triggers.

Uncle Richard tightened his stranglehold and Zeus gasped out, "Do what the American says!"

"Steve! Diana! Move it!" said Uncle Richard.

Still holding the HATE leader in front of him, Uncle Richard began moving up the slope away from the shore and toward the rocky highland in the center of the island. Stephen and Diana followed.

"Don't try to come after us," Uncle Richard shouted to the men, "if you value your leader's life."

Ten minutes later Uncle Richard, Stephen, Diana, and their captive were safely out of sight of their enemies. They climbed up through a desolate landscape of stones and twisted trees toward the top of the rocky spine of the island. From there they would begin their descent to the palace excavation.

"I'll make you pay for this," Zeus snarled as Uncle Richard pushed him along.

"Here's one more thing you can add to the bill," said Uncle Richard, wheeling him suddenly around and delivering a short, sharp karate chop to a nerve ending on the back of his neck.

Zeus slumped unconscious to the ground.

"He was slowing us down," said Uncle Richard.

"He'll wake up in twenty minutes or so. That'll give us a chance to get out of here."

"Then you've got a plan?" asked Stephen.

"Sometimes you just have to make things up as you go along," said Uncle Richard. He stopped to frisk Zeus, and came up with a pistol from a concealed shoulder holster. "There's one thing, though, I definitely plan to do. Get back our Kronoms."

Thirty minutes later Uncle Richard said, "There they are!"

Caked with sweat-soaked dust, Uncle Richard, Stephen, and Diana crouched behind a palace wall. Through a crevice they saw workmen carrying treasures down to a launch on the shore. From there the treasure would go to the trawler now anchored in the harbor.

Overseeing the workmen were two crewmen with rifles cradled in their arms.

And on the wrists of the crewmen the Kronoms gleamed.

"So near, yet so far away," said Uncle Richard, his jaw taut. "How do we get them?"

"I've got a plan," said Diana. "Quick, give me your gun."

Uncle Richard handed her the pistol he had taken from the HATE leader.

"Now, put up your hands and come with me," said Diana.

"I thought we could trust you," said Stephen. He

felt sick with disappointment. The sight of all that treasure must have swayed Diana back onto the side of the looters.

"Trust me," said Diana. "Look, they still think I'm on their side. I'll pretend to have captured you. When they come over to take you off my hands, I'll turn my gun on them without causing any commotion."

"I couldn't have come up with a better plan myself," said Uncle Richard, raising his hands.

Stephen did the same. His hands held high, they walked toward the crewmen with Diana following.

"Come and help me!" Diana shouted to the two crewmen with the Kronoms. "I caught the Americans in the ruins. They must have gotten off the yacht before it exploded."

"I guess they must have wanted their watches back," said one of the men with a grin as he came over to them.

"Yeah," said the other. "I'd give mine back, too, only they're not going to need them in just a little while. Time has just about run out for them."

"Hand over the watches, quick!" said Diana, turning her pistol on them.

"What the—" said the first crewman.

"Do what the lady says, dope," said the other. "Didn't your mother ever teach you manners. Never, never argue with a lady, especially when she's got a gun."

"Okay, okay," said the first. "The watch ain't no

good, anyhow. I never figured out how to make it do anything interesting, like add and subtract and stuff like that.''

The crewmen lay down their rifles and unstrapped their Kronoms. They held them out in their hands, and Uncle Richard and Stephen eagerly reached out for them.

''Drop it, lady,'' said a voice from behind them.

Stephen and Uncle Richard froze. Diana wheeled around and let her pistol fall from her fingers.

Four crewmen stood with rifles pointed at them.

''We were just coming back from hunting through the ruins to make sure no workmen were squirreling away any of the loot when we saw this dame had the drop on you,'' said one of them.

''What do we do with them?'' said another.

''You know our orders,'' said the first crewman as he picked up a Kronom. ''The Americans aren't supposed to live. And that's got to go for the lady here too.''

''How do we do it?'' asked the other crewman as he joined his companion in strapping his Kronom back on his wrist and picked up his rifle.

''Let's do it right,'' said the first. ''We can line them up by the palace wall. Then we can shoot them down, you know, like we're a regular firing squad. And I get to be the one who says 'Ready, aim, fire.' It's something I always wanted to do ever since I saw it in a movie when I was a kid.''

Stephen wondered what movie that was. He went through his vast memory file of movies and recalled a whole lot of them with firing-squad scenes. In most of them the good guys had been saved at the last minute.

But then he remembered the best and most realistic of them, *Paths of Glory*. Right up to the last minute he was sure the condemned prisoners would be saved, but they were shot down before his horrified eyes.

That was the movie he thought of now as he stood with Uncle Richard and Diana, their backs to the palace wall. The crewman had lined his companions up to form a ragged imitation of a firing squad. He had even offered Stephen and the others blindfolds before he remembered he didn't have any.

"He could have at least offered me a last cigarette," said Diana as the man walked back to rejoin the firing squad.

"Best he didn't," said Uncle Richard. "No sense in risking cancer."

"I'm sorry to have gotten you into this mess," said Diana. "But my plan did seem so terribly clever at the time."

"Don't apologize," said Uncle Richard. "Some of my plans don't work out perfectly either."

Then they both joined Stephen in terrified silence as the crewman in command opened his mouth with the relish of an actor about to deliver his juiciest lines.

"Ready! Aim!"

14

SACRIFICE TO THE GODS

FRIDAY: 4:40 P.M.
Ionia

"Stop it right there!" shouted a familiar voice.

It was Zeus.

He moved out of the palace ruins with his gun drawn, at the head of a group of heavily armed men.

"I knew you would head back for the treasure," he told Uncle Richard after the firing squad had been disarmed and placed among the other captives of the terrorists. "Greed will have been the undoing of all of you."

"I won't even try to convince you of our innocence," said Uncle Richard. "But I do have to thank you. This is the second time today you've saved us from an ugly death."

At this, Midas, standing under guard nearby, broke into a laugh that rumbled up deep from his belly.

"So Zeus has saved you from an ugly death?" he said when his laughter had subsided enough to let him speak. "Gads, sir, that is a good one. I must thank you for the last laugh I will ever have on earth."

"What do you mean, Midas?" asked Uncle Richard.

"You need only ask our red-haired friend here," said Midas. "I'm sure he will be only too delighted to tell you what he already has told me."

"Indeed, I will be *extremely* delighted," said Zeus. "It is one of my greatest ideas. Seeing the golden ax gave me my inspiration. That ax was used to make sacrifices to the mother goddess of the Minoans. Though I am a Greek and faithful to the Greek gods, I respect the divinities of the other great civilizations of the ancient world. It will give me great pleasure to pay homage to the mother goddess by offering her a fresh sacrifice—one much more precious than the animals that the Minoans used. This homage will be human blood."

"You can't be serious!" said Uncle Richard.

"You soon will see how serious I can be," said Zeus, returning Uncle Richard's look of shocked surprise with the burning gaze of a fanatic.

Zeus let his eyes move with leisurely contempt over Stephen and Diana, and Midas and his men. "You will also see how fair I can be. I will not take sides in the dispute between you two gangs of thieves. I will pick three sacrifices from each side—Midas, Apollo, and Stavros from one, and you two Americans and the Englishwoman from the other.''

His teeth gleamed white in the sunlight as he lifted his face toward the intense blue heavens above. ''O Mother Goddess, prepare for a feast such as you have not enjoyed for three thousand years!''

''What a kook!'' said Stephen as they were herded through the palace ruins.

''He's mad as a hatter,'' said Diana.

''Unfortunately, there's method in his madness,'' said Uncle Richard. ''He's taking us to the right spot for his scheme. The sacrificial courtyard.''

In the center of the courtyard stood a stone altar, a block of time-weathered marble on which animals had been placed. Still to be seen on the marble were shallow indentations carved thousands of years ago. They were gutters designed to drain off the blood.

Zeus placed an ancient urn with a design of flying birds on it to receive the blood. He stood with the golden ax in his hands beside the urn.

''Now we will select the order of the sacrifices in the honored Greek way, by lots,'' he announced.

He reached into the jar and pulled out a folded piece of paper.

''First, Diana Briggs.''

''Well, I suppose it's better than waiting and watching,'' said Diana.

"Next, Mr. Midas!"

"Gads, sir, this is . . ." said Midas, and ran out of words.

"Mr. Apollo."

"Hey, look, let's make a deal. I can give—" said Apollo, then realized he had nothing to offer.

"Mr. Stephen Lane."

"I guess this is one race against time we don't have to worry about," he said to Uncle Richard, trying to sound as cool as he wished he felt. "At least I won't have to explain why I haven't written my report on Greek ruins for school."

"Mr. Stavros."

"If I could just get my hands on you," Stavros said, and gave a grunt as the terrorist guarding him jabbed him sharply with a submachine gun.

"And last but not least, Mr. Richard Duffy."

"There's *got* to be some way out of this," said Uncle Richard. But when Stephen looked at him hopefully, Uncle Richard could say only, "If we had a little more time . . ."

But time had run out.

Diana was led to the altar with a guard on each side of her. Her hands were bound behind her back. Then she was forced to lie down upon the altar. She stared with fear-glazed eyes up at the sky, and then at the golden ax that Zeus slowly raised above her.

"If this were an ancient Greek drama," said Uncle Richard, gripping Stephen's shoulder to offer what reassurance he could, "a god would descend from the heavens to save her right now."

The ax reached the top of its rise, and an insane smile lit Zeus's face.

"But the Greek gods are long gone," said Stephen.

And he shut his eyes.

15

A FRIEND IN NEED

FRIDAY: 5:03 P.M.
Ionia

There was a buzzing in Stephen's ears, like a fly hovering near his ear.

It grew louder, and he opened his eyes.

Zeus stood frozen with the golden ax high over his head. He, along with everyone else, was looking out to sea.

Flying low over the sea toward the island came one helicopter, then another, and another, and another, until seven whirlybirds could be seen.

They were approaching at full speed. Within moments it was clear they were military craft, with the flag of Greece painted on their sides.

Uncle Richard didn't wait for them to land. He hurtled full speed toward Zeus.

This time Uncle Richard didn't use a flying tackle or a karate chop. He used an old-fashioned, unsophisticated punch directly on the tip of the jaw, with all the force of his arm, shoulder, and charging body behind it.

Zeus's head snapped back, and his body landed in a heap on the ground next to the ax he had been holding.

By now the lead helicopter had landed. Armed soldiers poured out the instant the skids touched ground.

Stephen recognized the first person out of the helicopter, the only one not in an army uniform, though he was carrying a military-looking .45 automatic in his hand.

Constantine.

The questions that came to Stephen's mind had to wait until the fight was over, but that didn't take long. In fact, there was barely a fight at all. Not a shot was fired. The terrorists could see that the military force was overwhelming. As if a vote had been taken, the terrorists threw down their weapons and started running right into the hands of more soldiers, who had landed on the other side of the island to cut off all retreat.

As Constantine said after the action was over and he sat with Uncle Richard, Stephen, and Diana in the professor's tent, "Capturing them all was much easier than I expected. On the other hand, I didn't expect it would be so hard a job sorting out our catch. Let's see, there are the terrorists, and the art thieves, and the assorted goons and petty crooks they hired to crew their yacht and do their digging. Am I forgetting anyone?"

Just then a soldier entered the tent and said, "One of our prisoners insists on seeing you. He claims he has valuable information."

"Send him in," said Constantine. "It's always amusing to see fellows like this try to wriggle off the hook."

Midas was brought in. His white suit was wrinkled and smudged with grime, his face had a five o'clock shadow, and his voice had shed all its charm and culture to reveal the hard and vicious streak beneath.

"If I'm caught, I don't want anyone getting out of this scot-free," he said, and pointed to Diana. "You can nab her, too, and I'll give you all the testimony you want that she was in with us."

Diana looked at Uncle Richard, who then exchanged glances with Stephen.

"Don't believe him," said Uncle Richard. "Diana only pretended to go along with the gang on my orders. I wanted a spy in the enemy camp, and it turned out I needed one. We owe our lives to Diana—a debt I can never repay."

"Oh, I think you've just done a rather good job," said Diana, relaxing.

"But I tell you, it—" said Midas angrily.

"I'm sure you'd tell me anything to get your revenge on Miss Briggs," said Constantine. "I suggest you forget about attacking innocent people and begin preparing your defense. You're going to need a good one if you hope to be free in less than seventy years."

After Midas was led away glaring, Stephen asked the inspector, "But how did you track the terrorists here?"

"It was simple, because we practically sent them here," said Constantine, smiling and taking a sip of the thick black coffee he had asked to have prepared as soon as the action was over.

"What do you mean?" asked Uncle Richard.

"I hope you don't imagine that our prisons are so poor that someone like Zeus could escape in a day," said Constantine.

"I *was* wondering about that," said Uncle Richard. Then his face brightened. "Now I understand."

"I still don't," said Stephen. "You two know more about this game of cops-and-robbers than I do."

"It's really quite simple," said Constantine. "We planted a police spy in the same cell as Zeus. Our man claimed to be a HATE supporter and arranged to have the leader and himself break out of jail. Then he told Zeus about the expedition to Ionia, and claimed that a gigantic art hijacking was under way. The leader did just what we hoped he'd do. He gathered the entire terrorist gang and headed by boat for the island, with our spy keeping up radio contact with us. We wanted to capture the entire HATE organization in one fell swoop and gave them enough rope to hang themselves."

"You almost gave them enough rope to hang *us,*" said Uncle Richard. "You timed your rescue much too close for comfort."

"Oh, *that,*" said Constantine, avoiding Uncle Richard's eyes. "I must admit, there was a slight delay in the arrival of our helicopter transport. It seems that the necessary papers hadn't been signed by the proper official, and we had to wake him up in the middle of the night before we could get things moving again. Sometimes, you know, even the best plans don't work out perfectly."

"Uncle Richard knows all about that," said Stephen, grinning.

"Still, all's well that ends well," said Constantine. "The criminals will soon be behind bars, and you are safe. And as a bonus, you have been treated to a side of Greece that most tourists never see."

"Oh, no!" said Stephen, suddenly grimacing.

"What's wrong?" said Uncle Richard.

"Something you ate?" asked Constantine.

"Something I didn't do," said Stephen. "The report on Ancient Athens I was supposed to write! I haven't even *seen* Athens, and there's no way I can fake it all from guide books. My history teacher is really sharp about stuff like that. He always demands eyewitness impressions as well as factual stuff."

"Perhaps you can stay here an extra week," suggested Constantine.

"No way," said Stephen. "One week of school is all I can miss, especially with finals to start preparing for. I have to take that Sunday flight, and it's already Friday night." He turned to Uncle Richard. "We'll have to come up with a real wild story this time, and I'm not sure it'll work. Mom and Dad have been acting more and more suspicious of the stories we've been telling them."

"Don't worry, Steve," said Uncle Richard. "Have I ever let you down?"

Stephen just stared at him.

"I said, don't worry," Uncle Richard said, and looked at the Kronom that once more was on his wrist. "We have more than enough time to see Athens. I have a plan."

16

THE GRAND TOUR

SATURDAY: 6:30 A.M.
Athens

"It's a sight few tourists ever see," said Constantine. "The Acropolis by sunrise."

"Especially by helicopter," said Stephen.

He sat in the bubble of an Athens police helicopter with Constantine at the controls, and Uncle Richard, Diana, and the professor beside him.

"It's the least the Greek government could do to repay your services," said Constantine. "True, I had to twist the arms of a few officials to make them approve this slightly irregular tour, but when I told them exactly what you and your Uncle Richard did, they were happy to oblige."

The helicopter landed on the Acropolis, the rocky

hill that dominated Athens. On it the ancient Greeks had built a complex of temples to honor their gods and goddesses. Chief among them was the Parthenon, the temple of the goddess Athena, one of the supreme human achievements of all time, now illuminated by the rising sun. Its tall, graceful columns seemed to soar into the pure blue sky.

"Let me be the first guide," said Diana, and took the Kronom that Stephen handed her.

"You don't have to hold it near your mouth. Just strap it on your wrist," he told her. "The recording function that I've activated is sensitive enough to catch everything you say."

Diana led Stephen and the others from temple to temple, and through the museum that Constantine opened with a special set of keys. The temples and statues were awesome, but Diana's words made them even more striking. The entire Acropolis came alive in Stephen's imagination as it must have looked to all who came to worship and wonder here two thousand years before.

From there they descended to the ruins of the Agora, the ancient marketplace where merchants once had traded goods while philosophers had exchanged ideas. Then they took a short helicopter hop to the towering, timeworn columns of the temple of Zeus and the magnificent arched gateway of the Roman emperor Hadrian near the center of the modern city.

The streets of Athens were filling with traffic and the

air with pollution as the helicopter rose high over the vast sprawl of the city. It sped northward until it was flying over fields cultivated by horsedrawn plows, pastures dotted with sheep and goats, and mountains thrust harshly upward by earthquakes long ago.

The professor took over the guided tour when the helicopter landed at the ancient sanctuary of Delphi.

He showed Stephen where the different Greek cities had built their treasuries in this holy place, safe from the ravages of war and the plundering of conquerors. He took them to the spot where the woman oracle went into her trances and issued her famous prophecies. Priests interpreted for people who came from all over the ancient world to learn what the future held. He told them how those priests set up the world's first international spying organization to gather the information that made their guidance so amazingly good.

Then he led them into the Delphi museum to gaze at the bronze statue of a young chariot driver found marvelously intact. Stephen stared at the erect, life-size figure with its hands lightly but firmly holding invisible reins and eyes staring eternally at the course that lay before it. He felt his pulse beat faster, as if that long-ago chariot race were still going on, speeding into the final stretch.

The next stop was the top of Mount Olympus, home of the Greek gods, where the ancient Olympic games were held, and the first modern Olympics took place. Constantine told them the story as they toured the ancient temples and the modern stadium where the grunts of the athletes and the cheers of the crowds still seemed to linger in the air.

By now it was late afternoon. Constantine hurried them aboard the helicopter to fly to a sight he did not want them to miss.

They landed at the end of a cape jutting into the sea in time to see the sun setting behind the temple of the sea god, Poseidon.

"Whew, what a day," said Stephen as he walked with the others back toward the helicopter. "I've learned more about history today than I have in my whole life."

"The day's not over yet," said Constantine. "I have another little surprise for after dinner."

They dined that evening in a Greek *taverna* where they went into the kitchen to choose what they would eat. Stephen played it safe with chicken. But after he had nibbled some of the roast lamb and honey-filled pastries the others had ordered, he wished he had been a little more adventurous.

"Now the surprise," said Constantine, and took them by government car to the National Archaeological Museum.

"I have received permission to take you through it tonight, though we cannot attract public attention by turning on the lights. We'll have to make do with flashlights."

''We've got something even better,'' said Uncle Richard. ''The watches that Steve and I have can produce all the illumination we need.''

By the light beams of the Kronoms, Stephen viewed century after century of artistic achievement, while Diana, the professor, and Constantine took turns in helping him see it clearly. He was still dazzled when he went to bed in Constantine's suburban villa late that night.

It seemed he had barely fallen asleep when he felt himself being shaken awake and heard Uncle Richard's urgent voice. ''Move it!''

17

TRAVELING LIGHT

SUNDAY: 8:30 A.M.
Athens

"We've overslept," said Uncle Richard. "I forgot to set my Kronom. We have to rush if we want to help Diana catch her flight and then catch ours."

Diana was packed and ready to go when they arrived at her room.

"You needn't have worried about me," she told Uncle Richard. "Archaeologists are used to getting up early—and an archaeologist is all I plan to be from now on. That's why I'm flying home to London now, to see if I can join an expedition about to set off for Peru. No more bright lights, champagne, or caviar for me. Just early to bed, early to rise, and good, hard, honest work at what I love."

"Glad to hear that," said Uncle Richard. He looked at her one small piece of luggage. "I see you like to travel light. You're a woman after my own heart."

"You know, I do think we're rather birds of a feather," said Diana, smiling at him warmly. "I mean, we do have the same taste for adventure. Why don't you join me in Peru?"

"I can see that we might make quite a team," Uncle Richard said, gazing into her eyes as if he were seeing a possible future together.

Stephen looked at his Kronom. "It's getting late. Constantine's waiting for us."

"Let me help you with that bag, Diana," said Uncle Richard gallantly.

"No, please, that isn't necessary," said Diana quickly. "As you said, it's really very light. I can handle it myself."

But Uncle Richard was too fast for her. He already had his hand on the luggage handle. He lifted it, then stood motionless.

He set the bag down and looked into Diana's eyes again, but in a different way.

"So this is what you call 'traveling light,' " he said. "I think we'd better open this bag to make sure something heavy hasn't gotten into it by mistake."

"Please, no, don't," said Diana.

"The key," said Uncle Richard in a voice that allowed for no argument.

"Please, let me explain," said Diana frantically.

Uncle Richard opened the bag, pushed aside some filmy clothing, and stared at what he had exposed.

"You see, I just wanted a souvenir of this adventure, and of you, Richard," said Diana in her sultriest, most appealing voice.

But Uncle Richard kept his eyes fixed on a spectacular jeweled golden Minoan sacrificial cup.

"I can see how much sentimental value it must have for you," he said. "About three hundred thousand dollars worth."

"I do need new archaeological equipment," said Diana. "Clothing, boots, cameras. I can't begin to tell you how professional expenses mount up."

"I don't think you'll need it where you're going," said Uncle Richard.

"Please," said Diana, her shoulders sagging.

Suddenly Stephen found himself echoing Diana. "Please, Uncle Richard."

Uncle Richard looked at him.

"I promised Diana that I'd remind you how much we owe her in case you forgot," said Stephen. "Now I'm keeping that promise. Besides, if you have her arrested, I guess you'll have to include me too."

Stephen took a small object from his pocket. It was a piece of marble. On it three letters were carved.

"I picked this up off the ground in Ionia," he confessed. "I always like to take home a souvenir from our adventures, and this seemed perfect. Except that now I know how valuable every little thing is in solving the mysteries of the past, even a couple of letters on a piece of marble.

"So you see, I was as bad as Diana. I couldn't resist picking up something ancient and walking off with it when there was so much simply for the taking. I can see why Diana gave in, whether you can or not."

Uncle Richard looked at Diana and then at Stephen. He grinned.

"I'll hand all your loot over to Constantine," he said. "And I'll tell him some story about forgetting we had it with us. He won't believe me, but he won't ask any questions as long as the finds wind up in the right hands. But I hope you've learned your lesson, Diana."

Diana put on her glasses and picked up her bag. "If you don't believe me, watch me when we get to the airport."

The first thing Diana did when they arrived at the airport was go directly to the ticket counter. She returned a few minutes later and showed her ticket to Uncle Richard and Stephen.

"I traded in my first-class seat for economy," she said. "Free Coca-Cola instead of champagne. I'm turning over a new leaf."

She paused as her flight to London was being announced.

"What I said about joining me in Peru still goes," she said to Uncle Richard.

"I might just take you up on that, just to make sure the treasures of the Incas stay put," said Uncle Richard.

Swiftly Diana flung her arms around Uncle Richard and kissed him. Then she planted a kiss on Stephen's cheek, picked up her bag, and walked out through the airport departure door and out of their lives—for the time being, at least.

18

THE HUNT FOR A HAPPY ENDING

SUNDAY: 6:30 P.M.
New York City

The first thing that Mrs. Lane said when Stephen and Uncle Richard came through the front door was "Don't tell me about it. I know everything!"

Both Stephen and Uncle Richard tensed.

"We got this just after you left," Mrs. Lane said.

She handed Uncle Richard a telegram, and Stephen read it with him.

It read: SORRY. CALLED AWAY ON SUDDEN BUSINESS. HOPE YOUR PLANS ARE NOT DISRUPTED. CONSTANTINE.

"Oh, *that*," said Uncle Richard, breathing out a sigh of relief.

"It didn't spoil your trip, did it?" asked Mrs. Lane.

''That would have been quite a waste of time and money,'' said Mr. Lane.

''Don't worry,'' said Uncle Richard. ''It all worked out.''

''Right,'' said Stephen. ''Constantine came back in time to save the situation. We got to see all the sights. Believe me, it was a week I'll never forget.''

''Remember, I expect you to write a good report on it for school,'' said Mr. Lane. ''I hope you took a lot of notes.''

''Even better than that,'' said Stephen. ''I have it all solidly recorded up here.'' He tapped his forehead, though it was his Kronom he was thinking of.

Then he said, ''Is it okay if I don't start writing it until tomorrow night? I'm kind of knocked out right now. I think I'll just wind down from the jet lag by watching a movie on my recorder, especially since there's one that I want to see again before my tape rental runs out.''

''What movie is that?'' asked his mother.

''An old one, *The Maltese Falcon*.''

''But you must have seen that at least a dozen times already,'' said his father.

''I know,'' said Stephen, ''but I want to see that fat actor who plays the chief crook one more time.''

''Ah, yes, Sydney Greenstreet,'' said his father.

''He was really quite good,'' said his mother. ''The very image of evil. He was so delightfully nasty you almost liked him.''

"And I especially want to see the ending again," said Stephen. "You know, where the hero has to decide whether to turn the girl he likes over to the cops because it turns out she's a crook. He turns her in, but I keep wanting to figure out if there was something else he could have done."

Then he turned to Uncle Richard. "Hey, want to watch it with me?"

"Sure," said Uncle Richard. "When it comes to figuring out the best thing to do in a tough spot, two heads are better than one."

"Thanks, Uncle Richard," Stephen said as their eyes met. "Thanks."

RACE AGAINST TIME ™